"How often do I have to tell you that I want you out of my life?"

"I don't think that's possible, Ellie. Even if I have to start all over again I'm going to make you fall in love with me."

"Keep away from me, Byron Meredith. Do you hear? Keep away!"

And with that she ran back toward the house. She wanted to free the love she felt for him more than anything in the world, but she could not, dared not, must never let herself get close to him....

Born in the industrial heart of England, **MARGARET MAYO** now lives in a Staffordshire village. She became a writer by accident, after attempting to write a short story when she was almost forty, and now writing is one of the most enjoyable parts of her life. She combines her hobby of photography with her research.

A Forbidden Marriage

MARGARET MAYO

DARK SECRETS

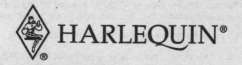

HARLEQUIN®

TORONTO • NEW YORK • LONDON
AMSTERDAM • PARIS • SYDNEY • HAMBURG
STOCKHOLM • ATHENS • TOKYO • MILAN • MADRID
PRAGUE • WARSAW • BUDAPEST • AUCKLAND

ISBN 0-373-80540-3

A FORBIDDEN MARRIAGE

First North American Publication 2000.

CHAPTER ONE

BYRON MEREDITH had always been proud of the building, so very proud, even though it wasn't the most prestigious he had designed. It was quite humble, in fact, by comparison. It had none of the glamour of the airport in northern Europe, or the Auriol Group's flagship hotel in South Africa, or any one of a number of designs that had won him international acclaim. His pleasure lay solely in the fact that he had given something back to the city where he had spent his student years.

As he still had a few minutes in hand before his meeting, he took the opportunity to study in turn each of the buildings on either side of the gallery, his eyes sharply critical. Then he turned his attention to the other side of the busy main street.

All of a sudden it was not the buildings that interested him but a woman in a pink short-skirted suit, her long red hair tied back at her nape. She was stunningly attractive, her head was held high and there was confidence in every stride that she took. She looked like a woman with a mission, glancing to neither left nor right.

Byron's heart gave a thud against his ribcage. Was he imagining things? Was she who he thought she was? It definitely looked like Ellie, a grown-up, sophisticated Ellie. But then, so had one or two other women, women with the same flame-red hair and the same pert little bottom. More than once he had made a fool of himself by running after them.

But this time he was sure. And he knew that he had to speak to her before she disappeared. Without a thought for the traffic, he stepped off the pavement and began what was to be a hair-raising journey across the road.

Two lanes of traffic streamed in both directions and none of the cars was prepared to give way. He dodged one only to find another directly in his path. Brakes screeched, horns blared, curses were thrown at him. He ignored them all.

Like a maniac he swerved this way and that, vaulting bonnets where necessary, stepping back a pace when it became clear that a vehicle was not going to stop, until finally, with more luck than judgement, he made it safely to the other side.

The woman in pink had almost turned the corner, and in desperation he called her name. He saw the look of shock on Danielle's face as she spun round. He saw the widening of her beautiful eyes, and her infinitely kissable mouth falling open.

'Byron,' she said huskily as he reached her side. 'You're the last person I expected to see. What brings you to Birmingham?'

'Business,' he announced briefly, dismissively. 'Lord, Ellie, you look good.' Which was the understatement of the year; she looked breathtaking. In a little under ten years she had matured from a pretty teenager into a ravishingly attractive woman. He couldn't imagine why he had ever let her go.

She didn't say, 'You too'; she simply stood and looked at him in silence. She looked stunned to see him—and not altogether pleased, which hurt like hell, though it was perhaps to be expected.

He wanted to tell her that she looked beautiful, but he didn't. Instead he said urgently, 'We must talk. Unfortunately I'm due in a meeting. Do you think we could get together later—for old times' sake?' She looked incredible, her porcelain skin glowing with good health. Even the freckles he had mercilessly teased her about looked entrancing.

Danielle shook her head. 'I don't think so. Old times weren't all that happy, were they?' Her clear, wide-spaced blue eyes looked into his slate-grey ones and dared him to refute it.

He had known she would refuse; all the time he had been leap-frogging cars he had known. It had been too much to hope that she would eagerly agree. Nevertheless disappointment knifed through him. 'Some of them were,' he remarked, and there was a similar challenge in the look he gave her.

'In the beginning maybe,' she acknowledged with a shrug. 'But we soon learned that we weren't compatible. Therefore I see no point.'

Byron made no attempt to hide his chagrin. 'I'm not expecting to make a habit of it, Ellie; I know that you've married again.' He saw the shock on her face and added quickly, 'I thought that it might be nice to talk, that's all, to find out what's been happening to you.'

'It's not something I wish to discuss,' she announced firmly. 'As far as I'm concerned the day we divorced was the day you no longer existed.' She looked as though there was something more she would like to add, but whatever it was she kept it to herself. 'I'm sorry,' she said instead. 'I also have an appointment to keep and I'm already late.' And with that she turned and walked away.

Byron found it hard to believe that she could do this to him. He wanted to go after her and talk some more. There were so many things he wanted to say; he simply couldn't let her go like this. He even took a couple of steps forward, his hand outstretched, her name on his lips—but his meeting with Summers was important, too important to ignore.

He stood and looked after her until she disappeared around the corner, and he kicked out at a nearby lamp-post in frustration. Dammit, he shouldn't have let her go; he should at least have suggested seeing her another time, when it was convenient to them both. Why the hell hadn't he?

It was not until later in the day when Byron got back to his hotel room that he had the chance to think again about Danielle. He took off his jacket and tie, loosened his collar, and flung himself down on the bed. With his hands behind his head he stared up at the ceiling.

He had met Danielle when she was eighteen and still at school studying for her A levels. He had been just twenty-one and at university. It was the university's annual rag day in aid of local charities, and he had held an improvised collecting box in the shape of a red plastic bucket under her nose and had refused to move until she put something into it.

'And if I don't?' she had taunted, flashing her incredible blue eyes at him.

'If you don't I shall tuck you under my arm and carry you back to my lair,' he had warned. And he'd been only half-joking.

Her red hair had caught his eye from several yards down the street and close up she had looked like a fragile china doll. He had instantly wanted to take her home—home being student lodgings at that particular time—and keep her for ever.

He had a thing about girls with red hair, probably because his grandmother had had red hair and he had happy memories of her cuddling him on her lap with her sweet-smelling hair tickling his face.

For over ten minutes he had stood talking to Danielle and at the end of it had fixed a date. That had been the beginning of what he had hoped would be a for-ever affair. But something had gone drastically wrong...

Danielle could not believe her eyes when she saw Byron waiting outside her house, leaning nonchalantly against an ice-blue Mercedes as though he had all the time in the world to spare.

She brought Sandor to a halt at his side, making no attempt to dismount, finding the extra height the horse gave her a definite advantage.

Meeting Byron yesterday had shocked her deeply; she had never expected to see him again, not after all this time. So much had happened, so much he knew nothing about, things she could never tell him.

It didn't matter that her pulses had quickened at the sight of him, that her heart had raced all out of sorts with itself. Her own feelings had to be kept well and truly hidden at whatever cost.

She had forged a new life for herself and had almost stopped thinking about him. Almost. It was not quite that easy, not when his name kept popping up in the newspapers.

Thinking about him had kept her awake for most of last night, and in a desperate attempt to clear her mind she had risen early and gone for a long ride. She'd thought it had worked—until she'd seen him outside her house.

'What are you doing here?' She deliberately made her tone cool. 'How did you know where I live?' Henley-in-Arden was eighteen miles from Birmingham; it could hardly be coincidence.

He looked taller and broader than in the days of their marriage, his designer suit a far cry from the chain-store shirt and jeans he had once used to wear. He exuded power and confidence now and total belief in himself.

His grey, thickly lashed eyes still held that seductive quality that made any girl want to go to bed with him. His short black hair had a scattering of grey at the temples, and there were tiny lines radiating out from his eyes, but they added to rather than detracted from his sex appeal. Even his voice was deeper, more sensual.

'I've known for a long time,' he admitted, patting the bay's neck as he spoke. 'A nice horse.'

'You have?' Further shock waves ran through her. How had he known? Why had he made it his business to find out? Apart from a few initial attempts to see her after she had left him and gone back to live with her parents there had been no contact between them. She'd thought that he must have pushed her completely out of his mind.

'Do you always go out riding this early?'

Danielle shrugged. 'Not always, but—I'm going out later.' She couldn't very well tell him that it was because she hadn't slept well.

'I see,' he said thoughtfully. 'So there's no hope that we could perhaps have lunch together? Or maybe even morning coffee?'

She was torn. One half of her wanted to spend time

with him, to find out what had been going on in his life—apart from what she had read in the papers. The other half saw no point in it.

Nevertheless she found herself nodding. 'Maybe coffee, here, if you can wait until I've seen to Sandor.' They would talk and he would be satisfied and then she would be rid of him.

Except that it wouldn't be easy disguising her feelings. Byron had always been able to arouse her every base instinct just by looking at her, and he was doing it again now. Those slate-grey eyes with those clear, clear whites, that too intent gaze, were sending a tremor through every bone in her body.

It had been so long and yet it seemed like only yesterday that they had flouted parental opinion and got married. They had given up school and got jobs—Byron as a builder's labourer and she as an assistant in a dress shop—and they had rented an old terraced house which they'd furnished scrappily with bits and pieces. They had been deliriously happy—to begin with.

'Let me help you.' He opened the gate to the paddock next to the house and closed it again after she had led the horse in. And after she had rubbed Sandor down and the horse had trotted off happily to join Danielle's mare, Morgan, Byron carried the saddle to the tack room and stood and watched as she cleaned it.

'Do you remember,' he asked, leaning back against the wall, thumbs tucked into his belt, his eyes lazily watching her, 'the plans we made to buy a house such as this, with a couple of horses in the paddock and a dog and a cat or two, and a few children as well?'

There was nothing in his voice to suggest that he was being sarcastic but Danielle felt quite sure that he was.

She kept her eyes down on the rein she was polishing. 'I guess it was not to be,' she said quietly.

They'd spent many happy hours making plans, especially when she'd discovered that she was pregnant. Naturally they hadn't intended starting a family so soon, but that hadn't stopped them being delighted. Particularly Byron. As an only child he had always promised himself that he would have a large family. He loved children, he had told her, and that was why they had talked about a big house in the country which he had wanted to fill with tiny feet.

When she had miscarried it had cut him up deeply. In fact he had blamed her for not looking after herself. She realised now that it was the inexperience of youth that had been talking, but at the time they'd had one hell of a row.

It had probably been the beginning of the downward spiral. That row had led to other rows—about money, or the lack of it, especially when Byron had been laid off during the winter months, rows about not understanding each other's needs, about all sorts of things that when she looked back on them were really very stupid.

She knew, however, that she had done the right thing in walking out on Byron when she'd discovered that she was pregnant a second time. She had been terribly worried that she might miscarry again—the doctors had warned her it could happen—and the thought of what it would do to her husband had scared her half to death. Reality had been even worse!

'Do you have children, Ellie?'

It was almost as though he had locked in on her thoughts. 'No,' she whispered, and hoped he did not see her sudden tears. Memories could be so savage.

And because she did not want him to ask any more questions she said, 'How about you, Byron? Have you married again?' He was the sort of man women died for, and she could not see him being short of female company for very long. He'd put on a few pounds but it was muscle not fat, and he looked better for it.

'No.' His answer was sharp and suggested that he was as loath to speak about that as she was about her childless state.

But she nevertheless persisted. 'Do you have a girlfriend?'

'Not in the sense you're suggesting.'

But he did have a friend who was female; was that what he meant? She wanted to ask more but guessed her questions wouldn't be welcome. And did it matter? After today she wouldn't see him again.

'I'm glad you went back to university.' When they first met he had told her that he wanted to be a great architect, he wanted to design buildings that would draw the admiration of the whole nation, the whole world even. He had succeeded beyond his wildest dreams. She had nothing but admiration for him in this respect.

'It was a good move,' he admitted. 'How about you? Did you finish your education?'

Danielle shook her head. There had been no chance of that, not when she'd suffered so badly from morning sickness that she had had to give up her job. 'I—er—carried on working,' she said, which she had done—eventually.

'But not for the same people.'

She frowned. Did he know all of her moves? Did he know about the baby? She went hot and cold at the thought. Was this the reason he wanted to talk to her now? Had she been wrong to agree to him staying for coffee? She rubbed vehemently at the strip of leather, only stopping when Byron laid his hand over hers.

'Ellie, did you really think I would forget you?'

She swallowed hard. 'I didn't expect you to know so much. I've not led such a high-profile life as you.'

'I was interested; I made it my business to find out. I also understand you've opened your own dress shop in Birmingham?'

She nodded. How much more did he know? Fingers crossed that it wasn't *everything*.

'Is it doing well?'

Danielle shrugged. 'Reasonably so.'

'I think you're being modest. City centre rates can be extortionate. I think you must be doing very well. Is it still your dream to open a whole chain?'

That had been her ambition—they'd both aimed high. She had even talked of designing some of the clothes herself. With a rueful smile she shook her head. 'I don't think so.'

It had been with great reluctance that John had let her open even one shop. He didn't want his wife working, he had said, having already insisted that she give up her job. But a housekeeper and a gardener left nothing for Danielle to do, and she had kept on about it until finally he had given way.

She had, however, conceded and let her friend Melissa run it for her, only putting in the occasional appearance herself. At least that was what John had thought. He had never known exactly how much time she spent there.

'You're content with your suburban little lifestyle?' The narrowing of Byron's eyes as he asked the question made Danielle frown. It was more than just a question;

there was something underlying it. Or was she mistaken? He knew so much about her that perhaps he also knew that she was now a widow. Was this another reason he had sought her out? Was he hoping that they could make a go of it second time around?

If so he was in for a big disappointment. It was an impossible dream.

'Yes, I am perfectly content,' she said firmly, 'and I think that's about it.' She hung up the reins and the saddle, took one last look around, and then led the way across the yard to the house.

She took off her riding boots outside the back door, and as they went in she wondered whether he would notice that it was furnished in the same way as they had once planned their dream home.

He'd remembered the big house, the paddock and the horses, but surely not the smaller details? She hoped not. John had given her carte blanche to do as she liked, and it had seemed like a good idea at the time to carry through her earlier plans. She had never dreamt that one day Byron would find his way here, or even that he would remember.

They went along the narrow hall and through the huge L-shaped lounge, furnished in restful shades of blue and grey accented with peach and yellow cushions and lampshades.

Byron seemed to hesitate as he looked around but Danielle resolutely carried on into the conservatory, where she pushed open the doors to the garden. The June sunshine was fragrant with honeysuckle and roses, birds were singing and everything was normal—except her heart rate! She was alarmed by the way her body was reacting.

Exotic plants had turned the room into a green jungle, and the cane furniture was heaped with soft squashy cushions in muted terracotta, green and blue. 'If you'd like to sit down I'll take a quick shower and change into something more comfortable.'

'That sounds promising.' His mouth widened into a wicked smile.

Danielle felt a moment's unease. She didn't want him getting any wrong ideas. 'Please don't forget that I'm married,' she retorted sharply.

'How could I forget? Those rings you're wearing must have cost a small fortune.' he said. 'But your husband's not here and I am.'

Unconsciously Danielle glanced down at the wide gold band of her wedding ring and the enormous diamond surrounded by sapphires that accompanied it. She didn't normally wear her engagement ring for riding, and couldn't think why she had jammed it onto her finger that morning. It had to be psychological.

They were a far cry from the cheap gold band Byron had bought her and which she still had in her jewellery box. But in her heart of hearts she knew that she treasured it the most. At least his comments proved that he did not know that John had died.

'I take it he won't be back until this evening?'

'Actually he's away,' she lied, and then wondered why she had not told him the truth; it was the perfect opportunity. She never lied. Lord, what was happening to her? 'Have you turned into the type of person who plays around with other men's wives behind their backs?' she asked sharply. 'Is that why you're not married?'

His grey eyes twinkled. 'There's only one man's wife

I'd—er—play around with, as you so wonderfully put it.'

'Then I'm afraid you're wasting your time,' she retorted, 'because this girl's not for playing.'

'You used to play beautifully.' His voice was a low, sexy rumble in his throat.

'When we were married,' she flung back. 'There is a difference.'

'Are you in love with your husband?'

Her eyes widened. 'What sort of a question is that, for heaven's sake? I wouldn't have married him if I wasn't. Now, if you'll excuse me...' And she quickly left the room.

Normally, after riding, she'd use the shower room next to the utility room, but this morning she ran upstairs and locked herself in her bedroom. Byron was unbelievable. He was surely not hinting that he wouldn't mind an affair? Was that why he was here? Had she made a fatal mistake, inviting him in? She grew hot as she stripped off her jodhpurs and shirt, swiftly followed by her bra and cotton panties.

The cool shower, usually refreshing, did nothing. She was still as hot and bothered when she stepped out of it. Damn the man. And she had thought it would be nice to talk! How badly she had misjudged him.

He'd never played these sorts of games before. When they'd been young, making love had been instantaneous and swift. No caressing her with his eyes, as he had done a few minutes ago. No exciting unspoken promises. No thought of holding back and making the whole experience so much more pleasurable.

When Byron had wanted to make love he had made love, and she, always as eager as he, had let him. She'd not had the experience to realise that half the fun of lovemaking lay in the preliminaries.

She roughly towelled herself dry, pulled on a silk shift in palest blue, ran a brush through her still damp hair, and ran lightly back down the stairs. She was in a hurry now to get rid of him.

In the kitchen she put the kettle on to boil and spooned coffee into the cafetière. She set cups and saucers out on the tray—bright yellow pottery ones that she always used for breakfast. They matched the rest of the north-facing kitchen with its light oak cupboards and its cheerful yellow curtains.

When there was nothing left to do but wait for the kettle she turned—and saw Byron standing in the doorway.

Her heart gave a jolt. She ought to have sensed him. Why hadn't she? How long had he been there? Perhaps only this instant. She hoped so. It was unnerving to think that he had been secretly studying her.

'It won't be long,' she said cheerfully, determined to hide the way her nerve-ends were skittering.

'There's no rush,' he answered, leaning nonchalantly against the doorjamb.

There was as far as Danielle was concerned. The sooner the coffee was made, the sooner they could drink it, and the sooner he would be gone.

'It's very nice.'

She frowned. 'What is?'

'Your house.'

Oh, dear! Had he been looking around in her absence?

'I'm pleased to see that your husband didn't inflict any of his ideas on you. This is exactly how you'd planned *our* house. I'm happy that you got what you wanted.'

Again she wondered whether there was a trace of cynicism in his voice.

'It's just a pity that we didn't share it together.'

'I'm surprised you remember,' she said quietly.

A dark eyebrow quirked. 'I remember everything, Ellie.' He pushed himself away from the door and walked slowly towards her. 'Everything.'

Danielle looked at him warily. Ought she to move? Back away? Make some pretence at finding something to do? How long before the kettle boiled? Why didn't it hurry up?

'Everything we've ever talked about, everything we've ever done.'

He was so close now that she could see the dark line which defined the slate-grey of his eyes, the enviably thick lashes, even the few white hairs which had dared to encroach into the crisp blackness of his hair. She thought he was going to kiss her—in fact she was sure of it, the intent was there in his eyes. And, knowing how fatal it would be, she quickly sidestepped and opened a cupboard door. 'Would you like a biscuit with your coffee?'

He smiled, aware of her panic, and resumed his position against the doorframe. 'No, thank you.'

Danielle's relief knew no bounds when the kettle came to the boil. She poured the steaming water into the cafetière and then picked up the tray. 'Right, shall we sit down?'

'I'll carry that.'

Reluctantly she gave it to him, but when his fingers touched hers—by design or accident she did not know—and set off a chain reaction that ripped through her whole body, she knew that the next half-hour or so was going to test her acting skills to the limit.

And the trouble was, she was no actress.

CHAPTER TWO

'I WANT to know exactly what you've been doing since I last saw you.' Byron sat with an ankle resting on a knee, his cup and saucer balanced in his hand. He wondered if Danielle knew what effect she was having on him. How quickly his heart was beating. How clammy his palms were becoming.

She gave a tiny shrug. 'There's not much to tell. My father died a few years ago.'

'I'm sorry to hear that,' he said. 'But that's not really what I'm asking.'

'There's nothing else.'

He raised his thick dark brows. 'You got married and opened your shop.' Lord, she looked good. He'd thought about her such a lot, he'd even dreamt about her recently, not once but several times. But reality was so much better than the dream. She was fantastic.

'But you know that. I've led a perfectly ordinary life otherwise.'

'How about those first few months when you walked out on me? What did you do then?' He couldn't understand why, if she had given up her job, she hadn't gone back to finish her education.

The day it had happened, the day she had left him, was a day that had lived in his mind for ever. At first he had thought she wasn't serious, that she would be back within a few hours. When she hadn't turned up he had been frantic, and finally, in desperation, after ringing all their friends, he had telephoned her parents.

21

He had hated having to do it and Evelyn Taylor-Garnham had taken great delight in informing him that her daughter was home for good, that she did not wish to speak to him now or ever again.

He had been gutted. Surely things hadn't gone that far? They'd had their ups and downs, he'd probably laid the blame on Danielle for things that weren't truly her fault, but surely they could have talked them through?

Each time he'd telephoned he'd got the same message, and when he'd called at the house her mother always answered the door and it had been impossible to get past her. He'd gone to Danielle's place of work only to be told that she had given up her job. And finally he'd had to accept that their life together was over.

'I went back to my parents,' she answered.

'I rather gathered that,' he commented drily. 'I did try to talk to you.'

'Yes, I know,' she admitted. 'My mother told me.'

And she'd let her mother be the front woman, he thought resentfully. Danielle had grown to hate him so much that she hadn't even wanted to speak to him. His lips tightened at the memory. 'What did your parents say when you went home? Was your mother absolutely delirious with delight?'

'She just thought we were too young,' said Danielle loyally.

'Really?' He could not keep the sarcasm out of his voice. Maybe that was part of the story, but not all. Her mother hadn't liked him; it was as simple as that. She hadn't approved of her only daughter marrying a penniless student. She'd thought him arrogant and loud and big-headed, and had had much better plans for Danielle. Mrs Taylor-Garnham was an out-and-out snob and her husband had been totally under her thumb. He had never said a word; he'd left everything to her.

'What did *your* parents say?' she countered.

He shrugged. 'They were sorry that it hadn't worked out. They said the usual things, like ''You youngsters never listen,'' ''Why do you always have to learn the hard way?'' et cetera, et cetera. But they were delighted when I told them I was going back to university. They're in America now; they went to join Uncle Joe last year. Why didn't you finish your education?'

'I had my reasons,' she said quietly, and he noticed that she avoided looking him in the eye. He wondered what those reasons were.

'You mean you preferred working to school?'

'Something like that,' she agreed.

'And you also found yourself a rich man and decided to divorce me.' He could not hide his bitterness now.

'It wasn't exactly like that,' she retorted defensively.

'As good as dammit,' he snarled. 'Did money buy you happiness?' All their married life she had harped on about money, or the lack of it. But he had never realised exactly how much it had meant to her.

He had gone looking for her again when he'd left university and got his first job. He'd had much better prospects then, much more to offer, and he'd still loved her. It had devastated him to find that she'd remarried. And hurt him even more when he'd discovered where she lived—the big house, the horses, the fancy cars—everything they had planned together.

'What is this, Byron, the third degree?'

'I just want to know.' Memories were tearing at his heart, renewing his anger at the unfair way she had treated him. 'It's important to me.'

'Why?' she asked sharply.

'Isn't it obvious?' His grey eyes glittered warningly. 'According to you, money was always at the root of our problems.'

'That was part of it,' she agreed, 'but not all. Our parents were right—we were too young. We thought of ourselves all the time; we each wanted our own way. Give and take didn't enter into it. We were totally selfish.'

'Were we?' he asked, an eyebrow arched. But he knew she was right. They *had* been too young; neither of them had been ready for marriage. Neither of them had realised how much money it took to run a home. They should have heeded their parents' advice and waited until they had finished their education and were in decent jobs.

'As a matter of fact,' she said, answering his earlier question, 'I am happy, extremely happy.' And she neatly turned the tables by adding, 'How about you?'

Was he happy? Byron had never asked himself that particular question. When he'd found out about Danielle marrying again he'd had difficulty in coming to terms with it. He'd dated more women than he could remember, he'd drunk far too much, and in general had made a terrible mess of things.

But he'd gradually come to his senses, telling himself that she wasn't worth all the heartache. Now he was doing very well for himself. So he must be happy, mustn't he?

'I lead a good life,' he conceded.

'But there's no one special in it?'

His mouth turned down expressively. 'Maybe I'm not interested. Maybe there's a certain person who's spoilt me for anyone else.' It was true. He had never found anyone who had captured his heart the way Danielle had.

There was Sam, of course, and he was fond of her, but he didn't love her—not the way he loved Danielle. Sam was more of a friend than anything else, a mate, a buddy, someone he could talk to...

Danielle drew her brows together into a disbelieving frown. 'You're surely not suggesting that your unmarried state has anything to do with me?'

'I'm not suggesting that at all,' he said. He had to be careful; he was giving too much away.

'Then what are you saying?'

'That for the moment I'm content with the way things are.' Which was a definite untruth. Twenty-four hours ago he had been content, but not since he had seen Danielle and spoken to her. Too many memories were being dragged to the surface, his mind was in turmoil, and he had no idea where it was all going to end.

'The newspapers are saying that you're a second Joseph O'Flannery.'

Byron pulled a wry face; he was well aware of how the media exaggerated. 'I don't know about that. He was one of the greatest architects that ever lived. I was privileged to work with him. I was invited to stay on with the firm when he died but I decided to go it alone.'

'And now you're an international success, renowned for taking chances, for your foresight and visionary concepts. You're a man much in demand, Byron. You must feel pretty good about it. If we'd stayed married you'd never have realised your ambition.'

'I'd have got there one day,' he claimed. 'Have you been keeping tabs on me as well?' The thought pleased him enormously.

But Danielle shook her head. 'It's what I've read in the papers. Where do you live now?'

It was encouraging that she was asking questions. At

least it proved that she wasn't totally uninterested. 'My main home is in London, a penthouse in Maida Vale. But I have a small apartment in France as well, as I do a lot of work in Europe, and a holiday home in St Lucia.' More than anything he would like to take her there, to swim in the crystal-clear waters with her, to sit out beneath the stars, to just be with her, the two of them alone.

He saw the way her brows rose, the surprise, and the pleasure too. He had feared for a moment that she might think he was bragging, that she might not be pleased for him. But she was; it was there in her beautiful blue eyes.

'I'm impressed,' she said. 'You've done even better than I thought. I felt really proud when I heard that you'd been asked to design the new gallery in Birmingham to house the Granville Archer collection.'

'And what a collection,' said Byron.

The whole nation had been intrigued when Granville Archer had died and left his treasures to the city. Paintings by Canaletto and Renoir and other past masters, thought lost to the country for ever, had been discovered. His whole house had been filled with unique works of art, with silver and porcelain and china, all of it rare, some of it packed away in boxes, not having seen the light of day for years.

'Is it true that his neighbours had no idea?'

Danielle nodded. 'None at all. He was once a businessman, but for many years had been a recluse. He'd never married, didn't even own a car. If he went out a taxi came for him, but that wasn't very often. And he had no family. He didn't even leave any money, not a significant amount, anyway, just about enough to bury him. Isn't it sad?'

'Very much so,' agreed Byron. 'And I'm glad that the City of Birmingham decided to honour him. And proud that they asked me to design the gallery. It was good coming back.' What he didn't tell her was that it had evoked memories that had never really gone away, and that he had constantly hoped and prayed that he might bump into her.

'The newspapers have told me nothing about your private life.' Danielle lifted a questioning brow.

'That's because I don't have one,' he told her. 'I live for my work; I'm a very busy man. I get involved in all aspects of it. I don't stand back once the design part's done, I take an active interest in the building work as well. There are plenty of unscrupulous people around who could damage my reputation. I know everything's supposed to be checked and double checked, but you can't be too careful.'

'I know,' she said, surprising him. 'John's told me all sorts of horror stories.'

'Your husband's in the building trade?' This was interesting. Byron had deliberately not probed too deeply into Danielle's marriage. Apart from discovering that she'd married someone named John Smith and that they lived south of Birmingham in the pretty market town of Henley-in-Arden, whose long main street was lined with oak-timbered buildings several hundred years old, he had kept himself in ignorance.

Not because he wasn't interested—he was, most definitely. He had desperately wanted to know what type of guy Danielle had chosen to marry second time around. But he knew that if he ever came face to face with him he would be unable to keep his fists to himself. It was therefore best, he had reasoned, that he knew nothing.

'Yes,' she answered, 'he is.'

Reluctantly answered, he thought. 'How did you meet him?'

She looked even more uncomfortable. As soon as she spoke he knew why.

'I worked for him,' she admitted quietly, hesitantly. 'I took a secretarial course and Melissa's sister—you remember my friend Melissa?—she put in a word for me.'

'So it was your boss you married!' It hurt, it hurt deeply, to think that Danielle had become so mercenary. Money had been behind a lot of their quarrels, but even so...

'Why doesn't it surprise me?' he asked, unable to keep a scathing note out of his voice 'And how about children? Wasn't it four you said you wanted? Why have you never carried out that part of your dream world as well?' Lord, he was angry now and it was impossible to hide it. It was time he left, before he said something he regretted.

'I don't see that it's any of your business.' Danielle's tone was terse as she glanced down at her watch. 'Time's flying, Byron; I do have to go out.'

He grasped the excuse, finished his coffee and put down the cup. 'Maybe we can meet again before I go back to London?' When he had calmed down, when he could speak to her without castigating her for marrying for money.

Danielle shook her head. 'I don't think so.'

'You mean this is it?'

'Yes.'

'That's a pity.' His eyes locked into hers. Maybe Danielle didn't want to see him ever again, but he most definitely wanted to see her.

*   *   *

Long after Byron had gone Danielle sat and stared into space. She hoped he would take her at her word and not get in touch again. There was so much about which he knew nothing, and it was best it remained that way.

She had been right to leave him. It wasn't hard to imagine how he would have reacted. She had been so happy when she didn't miscarry, so deliriously pleased when baby Lucy was born. She had even been planning in her mind to go back to Byron, knowing he would welcome them both with open arms, and had been plunged into the depths of despair when she'd been told a few hours later that the baby had died. She had thought she would never get over it.

And worse was still to come. When the doctor had taken her to one side and in a kind, gentle and sympathetic voice explained that she would never be able to have another baby, she had thought her life was over. And she knew that if she hadn't already left Byron he would have most definitely left her. She was no good to him if she couldn't give him children.

She had sat at home for many long months doing nothing—except waiting for her divorce. She had filed for it straight away. No matter how much she would have liked to go back to Byron she couldn't commit him to a childless marriage.

Eventually she had let Melissa persuade her into taking a secretarial course at the local business college. Why a secretarial course she had not known; it was something she had never thought about. But Melissa had insisted that she would earn more money than working as a shop assistant. And, once qualified and installed in a job at JBS Developments, Danielle had found that she quite enjoyed it.

She'd done well and in no time became the managing

director's personal assistant, and when eventually she became his girlfriend too she'd felt that her life was back on an even keel. John Bryan Smith had actually owned JBS, and marrying him had been a big decision. Only the fact that he'd said he definitely didn't want children had finally persuaded her.

She had not loved him as completely as she'd loved Byron, and there had been more than one occasion when she had wished it were Byron lying in bed beside her. John had sometimes grown impatient with her lack of response, and had accused her of being frigid. Eventually he had stopped making love to her altogether. But they'd remained good friends and had been happy enough together. When the accident had happened she had been truly distraught.

And eleven months after John's death she'd met Tony Cochran. Darling Tony, a big bear of a man, warm-hearted, caring, the kindest person you could ever wish to know. He was a father-confessor type and she had told him about Byron, more than she had ever told John. She'd told him everything, in fact, and he'd had all the time in the world to listen. A few weeks later he'd asked her to marry him. She'd repeatedly said no but he remained equally persistent.

He was in Malaysia now. He was an engineer and his company had sent him out there for six months to train some of their workers. He had said, when he'd accepted the job, that it would give her time to make up her mind.

Danielle knew her answer would still be no; Tony was far too nice a guy to be lumbered with a sterile wife. But she couldn't deny that he was good for her. He had restored her sanity, he made her laugh and he made her feel good about herself, he was great fun to be with. She had begun to enjoy life once again—until Byron had turned up! She wished Tony were here now. She could do with his down-to-earth humour.

It had definitely been a mistake inviting Byron in. She could still feel him, smell him; it even felt as though she could reach out and touch him. It would be difficult now to get on with her life and not imagine him here.

That weekend Danielle was away from home taking part in some horse trials, and she was feeling particularly pleased with herself when she got back late on Sunday. She was tired but she had done well, and the main thing was that she had managed to forget Byron.

She was looking forward to a long, relaxing bath, a bite of supper, and then bed—until she found the note pushed through her letter box. Instantly all thoughts of food and sleep fled.

Dinner on Wednesday.

Seven o'clock.

That was it. No signature, nothing. But the bold black handwriting was all too familiar. And she could blame no one but herself. The lie that John was away had caught her out.

She didn't want dinner with Byron, not on Wednesday, not on any day. And how typical of him to assume that she would accept. Had she known his hotel, she would have phoned and told him so. She didn't even know his London address. Maida Vale, he had said, but her curiosity had already led her to check the phone book, and she'd found no Byron Meredith listed, not even a business address for Byron Meredith, architect.

It looked as though she was stuck with the date

whether she liked it or not. He would turn up and expect her to be ready. She could be out again, of course. How was he to know that she hadn't gone away for a whole week or even longer? But that was the coward's way out.

When the telephone rang her heart lurched. If it was Byron she would take great pleasure in telling him that he had assumed too much, that she wouldn't date him under any circumstances.

But it wasn't her ex-husband, it was her mother, reminding her they were having lunch together tomorrow. Danielle wondered what her mother would say if she told her that Byron had popped back into her life. It wasn't hard to imagine.

On Wednesday Danielle found herself dressing with extra care. Right until the last minute she had been determined not to go. She had planned to wear jeans and a T-shirt and tell Byron that he was wasting his time.

So what had made her change her mind? She could find no answer.

At seven on the dot he rang the bell. Danielle opened the door and every sense reached to him. In a dark lounge suit with blue shirt and grey patterned tie he looked every inch the prosperous businessman he was; he also looked incredibly sexy, and she could not stop her heart racing. It was unbelievable, the sensations he aroused in her.

She invited him in.

'You look stunning, Ellie.' His appraisal was thorough.

She had chosen to wear a deceptively simple grey silk dress that skimmed her curves, hinting at what was beneath but giving nothing away. And as his eyes slowly took in every inch of her, right from the tip of her silver sandal-clad feet, up over her slender hips and flat stomach, lingering slightly on her breasts, she felt the beginning of a meltdown. She shook her head briefly to try and dispel it.

'You took a chance, Byron.'

'I realise that, but it was worth it.'

As he pulled out of the drive Danielle did not dare ask where he was taking her; she wasn't sure that she could control her voice. Things were happening to her senses that she didn't want to happen. This was going to be a big mistake.

She most definitely ought to have been out. She ought never to have agreed to this insane date. And as the minutes ticked away, as he drove beside her in infuriating silence, a smile playing about his generously wide lips, she became more and more sure of it.

When he turned onto the approach road of a tiny private airfield she frowned and finally spoke. 'Byron, where are we going?'

He continued to smile but said nothing.

'Byron?' she asked more urgently.

But again he didn't answer.

Finally he stopped the car, helped her out, and escorted her to a waiting Lear jet.

Danielle thought she must be dreaming. 'What is this? I thought you were taking me out for dinner. I'm hardly dressed for—'

'We *are* eating out,' he informed her.

She frowned. 'I don't understand.'

His annoying smile widened. 'How does dinner in Paris sound?'

CHAPTER THREE

'I CAN'T believe that I'm actually sitting here with you.' Danielle looked across the table at Byron. 'I think I must be dreaming.'

'It's no dream,' he assured her, his grey eyes warm as he reached out and placed his hand over hers. 'Feel me; I'm very real.'

Danielle wanted to snatch her hand away. They had been sitting in a tiny elegant French restaurant for over an hour now, and with each minute that passed she became more and more aroused. It was as though the last ten years were being gradually wiped away. Just looking at Byron excited her and the longer they sat, the more difficult it was to take her eyes off him.

She had thought he was good-looking when she married him but he was doubly attractive now—dangerously so in fact. Heads had turned as they'd walked into the restaurant and there had been many more both discreet and indiscreet glances in his direction as the evening progressed.

Success sat well on his shoulders. It showed in the way he dressed, in the unconsciously arrogant way he held himself—his arrogance was what her mother had hated most. Everything about him shrieked power. And combined with his devastating sensuality it stirred her senses as nothing else ever had.

When his fingers tightened around hers she realised that she had left it too late to move.

'You *are* enjoying yourself, Ellie?' He sounded suddenly anxious, as though it was important to him.

'I guess I am.'

'But you're not sure?'

The warmth from his hand reached every corner of her body, creating the sort of tingling sensation she had not felt in years, had actually never felt with anyone except him.

'I've never been treated like this before,' she said huskily. 'I've never been whisked away to Paris for dinner.' It was incredibly romantic and a far cry from the cheap cafés he had used to take her to.

'You've no idea how good it is to see you again.' His smile was hungry, as though it was her he would prefer to be eating rather than the food on their plates. 'I truly thought it would never happen.'

'You mean you've been wanting to seek me out all these years?'

He nodded unashamedly, his dark grey gaze raking every inch of her face. 'Don't tell me that you haven't thought about me too?'

'My fish is getting cold,' Danielle pointed out.

But he didn't let her go. 'I can't believe that I've not occupied a tiny corner of your thoughts.'

She shrugged. 'Maybe—just occasionally.'

'But not enough to warrant getting in touch with me?'

Her eyes widened. 'I couldn't have done that even if I'd wanted to.' And, finding her hand suddenly free she picked up her fork and prodded it into her sole meunière. Not that she felt like eating now.

'Why is that?'

'Because I didn't have your address. Unlike you, I haven't pried into your private affairs.'

He pretended to look hurt. 'That's unfair.'

'Is it?' she asked, her finely shaped brows rising. 'I don't like the idea that you knew all along where I lived.'

'I ought never to have let you go.'

'There's no point in thinking that now,' she said, unaware that there was a sudden sharp edge to her tone. 'What is done is done; we cannot change it.' She took a tiny mouthful of fish, but instead of melting in her mouth it now tasted like cardboard.

'They've been long years.'

'I can't imagine why you never remarried.'

He shrugged. 'Like I said, you were my first and only love.'

'But you must have had girlfriends over the years.' He was too virile a man to have remained celibate.

'Naturally.'

'And was there not one you wanted to spend the rest of your life with?'

'No.'

'I find that hard to believe.'

'Maybe I never stopped loving you.' His eyes locked with hers.

Danielle felt a tremor of unease.

'Maybe I never found anyone who excited me as you did—as you still do, Ellie,' he added urgently, gruffly. 'Did you know that?'

She shook her head, too stunned to speak. What was he trying to say?

'It's almost as though we've never been apart. Do you feel that way too?'

Again Danielle did not answer. She swallowed hard and gave a further tiny shake of her head. It was too dangerous to admit that the feelings running rampant within her were entirely due to his presence, feelings that were magnified many times over compared to what they used to be.

'Ellie.' He put down his knife and fork and looked at her gravely. 'It was the biggest regret of my life, the day you walked out. Why wouldn't you even speak to me when I phoned? When I came to the house?'

'There was no point.'

'You fell out of love with me, just like that?'

Danielle drew in a deep breath and expelled it slowly. 'I knew it was over,' she said, avoiding his eyes, playing with her fork instead.

'How could you have been so sure?'

'Things had been going downhill for months, Byron. You know they had. We seemed to do more arguing than anything else. Do you remember the time I came home with a new pair of shoes and you hit the roof because the electricity bill was unpaid?'

'Yes, I remember,' he said quietly. 'I thought about it afterwards. I was wrong. You needed those shoes for work. I behaved like an idiot most of the time. And more especially when I blamed you for losing the baby. I didn't know what I was saying. It's just that I wanted that baby so badly. It was part of me, part of us, and I think it would have made a difference to our marriage.' He shook his head as though trying to banish the memory. 'Do you forgive me, Ellie?'

'I guess so.' It crucified her to hear him say these things. It proved beyond a shadow of doubt that they had no future together.

'Can we be friends again?'

Danielle shook her head. 'There is no point.'

'Why?' His thick brows drew into a straight, enquiring line. 'Because I live so far away? Because I travel a lot? Because you're married?'

'Just because,' she said. 'I'd really rather not talk about it. Tell me what you're doing in Birmingham. You said business—what sort of business? Have you been asked to design something else?'

She thought for a moment that he was not going to answer, that he was going to continue to press the issue of them seeing each other.

It was a relief when he finally said, 'It's to do with the Granville Archer Gallery. There are one or two problems; someone's not done their job properly. But no one knows about it yet.'

Danielle frowned. 'Can you tell me?'

Byron shook his head. 'Tonight is a special occasion; I don't want to spoil it with talk about work.'

'But I'm interested,' she insisted. 'You're forgetting I know a bit about the building trade.'

'Of course.' His grey eyes grew suddenly thunderous. 'I'd almost forgotten that your husband's a builder. A damned rich builder.'

He sounded so disparaging that Danielle was forced to leap to John's defence. 'Actually he was a property developer. JBS is highly regarded in the industry.'

The second she spoke Danielle knew that she had made a colossal mistake. JBS had handled the gallery project! Byron would make the connection. A chill stole over her until her whole body grew so cold that she began to tremble.

When she'd heard years ago that Byron was designing the new gallery, and when John had been handed the contract, she'd had fears that the two men would meet. She'd constantly prayed that neither of them would find out who the other was. And they hadn't.

Thankfully she had never talked to John about Byron. She had simply told him that her first marriage had been a mistake and that she wanted to forget it. He had never questioned her.

She could almost hear Byron's mind working now, and her fears were realised when he scraped back his chair and jumped to his feet. 'Let's get the hell out of here. You and I have a lot of talking to do.'

Byron's meeting with JBS Developments was not going well. Bruce Summers, the surveyor, was supposed to have been present but he had not yet turned up and Rod Maston's phone kept ringing. It was going to be one of those days.

He strummed his fingers on the desk and glanced again at his watch. Eight-thirty-five. Six hours and twenty minutes exactly since he had taken Danielle home. He had not arranged to see her again but he intended going round this evening with a bottle of champagne and a basket of strawberries.

They would sit in her garden and he would feed them to her one by one; he would watch her infinitely kissable lips part, her tantalising little tongue accept the succulent fruit—and as he watched her his adrenalin would surge, as it was doing now at the very thought, and he would want to cover her mouth with his own; he would want to taste her as she was tasting the strawberries.

Except that he had to tread carefully. He was well aware that she was not yet ready to accept him back into her life.

They had walked along the Seine after leaving the restaurant, dusk softening the edges of the beautiful stone buildings, lights transforming the whole scene into a place for lovers. He had taken her hand and felt how tense she was. He had said softly, carefully, 'Why didn't you tell me?'

It had come as a hefty shock to discover that it was John Smith of JBS that she had married, because he knew very well that John had died nearly two years ago. So why was she pretending that her husband was still alive? For protection? From some people maybe; some people saw widows as easy game. But from him?

She had shaken her head and said nothing.

'I know it must be hard to talk about him,' he'd gone on, squeezing her hand encouragingly. 'It was a terrible accident and must have upset you deeply.'

He had been out of the country when it had happened. John had apparently gone into a hard-hat area without the necessary headgear. A labourer high on the building had somehow lost his footing and dropped a hod full of bricks. Despite everyone yelling at John to get out of the way he had not been quick enough. He had died in hospital a few days later.

'How long would it have been before you told me?'

Danielle had given a tiny shrug of her narrow shoulders. 'When the time was right.'

Which had been no answer at all. The time would have been right a week ago, when he'd seen her in the city, when he'd first gone to her house. 'Do you find it difficult to talk about him?'

She'd nodded and he'd seen the glint of tears in her eyes, and it had hurt like hell to think that John's death still upset her. She must have loved him very much. Perhaps more than she had ever loved him. Nevertheless there was hope now where there had been none before, and—

'Have you heard a word I've said?'

Byron came back to the present with a start. 'I'm sorry?'

'That was Bruce on the phone,' said Rod. 'Something

urgent's cropped up; he can't make it.' Rod was a small, wiry man with boundless energy, and his washed-out blue eyes were fixed on Byron.

'Damn!' Byron swore explosively. 'So it's you and me.' It had taken him so long to pin this man down that he was not going to put the meeting off.

He pushed Danielle decisively out of his mind. 'What I want to know is why those cracks have appeared. I want you to take me step by step through everything. Here are my original plans. I want to know if they were followed exactly, if other materials were used instead of the ones I stipulated. I want to know if the foundations were the correct depth. It's my belief that this whole thing is caused by subsidence. We had one hell of a dry summer last year.' He thumped his fist on the desk. 'I made provisions for such an eventuality. It should never have happened.'

The meeting lasted the whole morning, but the instant Byron left the offices of JBS Danielle was back in his mind. It was ironic that she had once worked here, he thought, pausing to glance back at the red-brick building with its name in handsome gold lettering. Even more ironic that it now belonged to her.

He'd been here several times in the early stages of the development, he'd even met her husband. A very private individual, not the type to have a photograph of his wife on the desk, or to talk about what he'd been doing the night before.

Byron hadn't particularly liked him; he'd thought him rather a cold fish. The sort who lived for his work, and to whom the people around were merely parts of a well-oiled machine. Obviously Danielle had found a different side to his character, otherwise she would never have married him. She was a warm, sensual, exciting woman, and she would not have married anyone who could not meet her demands.

He was selfishly glad that she'd had no children. He wanted any children she bore to be his. He wanted lots of children.

He thought of her soft, sweetly scented body against his, he thought of himself inside her, and his hormones raced. He couldn't wait for this evening. He'd spent so many agonised nights after she'd walked out on him, the torture of it had never really gone, and now he wanted her back in his life again—permanently.

It was only half past six when he rang her doorbell. He'd sat in his hotel room watching the clock, and then the horrifying thought had struck him that she could be going out and if he left it any longer he might miss her. It had sent him running for his car.

And, Lord, how beautiful she looked. Her cheeks were flushed, her hair hung in crisp, damp tendrils around her face and shoulders, looking almost brown instead of its usual flame-red. She was dressed in a blue silky kaftan that exactly matched the colour of her eyes. He grew very agitated when he realised that she had nothing on underneath.

'Byron!' She was clearly amazed to see him.

'I thought we could share these.' He held out the wine and the plump, juicy fruit, and kept his fingers mentally crossed that she had no other plans.

She frowned and said sharply, 'Didn't I make it clear that I want nothing further to do with you?'

He hid his disappointment. 'Yes, but I had no one to share the champagne with.' And in his most pleading voice, 'Have you any idea what it's like, sitting alone in a hotel room night after night?'

She smiled then, reluctantly, and he knew he had won. 'But you're not to make a habit of it,' she warned as she stepped back for him to enter. 'And I'm not actually sure about drinking champagne on an empty stomach.'

'That can easily be remedied,' he said. 'I haven't eaten either. We'll have supper together; I'll help you make it.'

'I'm not even decent!' she exclaimed. 'I haven't long come out of the shower.'

'You look beautiful.' He did not realise that his voice had dropped a couple of octaves, that it came out as a low, sensual growl, that he was making it as clear as the nose on his face that he found her immensely fanciable. 'Can I put this champagne in your fridge?'

'Of course. I'll just pop upstairs and get dressed.'

He didn't want her to do that; he wanted her to sit and talk to him exactly as she was. He wanted to imagine her naked body beneath the robe...

'Ellie, stay as you are.' The plea was out before he could stop it.

She turned at the bottom of the stairs, her blue eyes wary.

'You look—you look as you did on the day we first met,' he said. 'Very innocent, very lovely.'

'You're saying that ten years hasn't aged me?' she asked with a tiny, nervous laugh.

'Not in my eyes. You're still the same; you're still my Ellie.'

He heard her cry of distress as she ran up the stairs and he realised that he would have to be more careful. Winning her love a second time was not going to be easy.

After putting the champagne in the refrigerator, he returned to the bottom of the stairs, sitting on the chair that faced them. Five minutes later Danielle came back down, the kaftan replaced by a pair of loose silk trousers in deepest cinnamon and a cream short-sleeved blouse which buttoned right up to her neck. He could have wept. It was as though she had deliberately covered herself up.

An hour later they were sitting out on the terrace eating spicy chicken and salad and crusty French bread. The champagne was nestling in an ice bucket beside them and the strawberries sat glistening invitingly in a white china bowl.

'A feast fit for a king,' he remarked. Danielle had relaxed as the minutes ticked away, as they'd stood side by side in the kitchen preparing their meal. He had wanted to say that it was like old times, but he hadn't dared. He had wanted to say a lot of things but had been fearful of spoiling their momentary rapport.

When they were ready for their strawberries he put the bowl between them, filled their crystal flutes with the bubbling champagne, and proceeded to do exactly as he had planned.

At first Danielle laughed and pulled away when he tried to feed her, but then she took one of the strawberries between her even white teeth and bit it in half. Some of the juice ran over her lips and he watched in fascination as she licked it off with the tip of her delicate pink tongue.

He would have done that for her, had she allowed it. In fact he desperately wanted to kiss her, and it took all of his self-control to remain seated. As he continued to feed her so did his need of her deepen, so much so that in the end he got out of his chair and took a walk around the garden.

Honeysuckle sweetened the air, bees droned, a single

aeroplane drew a white line in the sky. Maybe he could organise a plane to write 'Ellie, I love you.' It was a fleeting, impractical thought. The sun continued its descent. He was pleased when Danielle joined him, champagne glass in hand. 'I love this time of day, don't you?' she asked huskily.

'It's my favourite,' he agreed.

'Do you have a garden in London?'

He nodded. 'A roof-top garden. Everything's grown in containers.'

'How interesting.' Danielle's face lit up. 'Who looks after it when you're not there?'

'Sam, my neighbour.' She did it willingly because she was a little in love with him, even though he never gave her any encouragement. He had made it clear that he wanted nothing more than friendship.

He wanted to say that he would show his garden to Danielle one day, but knew that it was too soon. 'This is pretty, Ellie.' He looked around at the neatly manicured lawns and colourful flowerbeds. 'Do you have help?'

She shook her head. 'I do it myself mostly. We used to have a gardener but I got rid of him, and now I only get a man in if I need any heavy jobs doing. I enjoy it.'

'I remember when you didn't know one flower from another.'

'Nor was I interested,' she agreed with a smile. 'Going to discos and having a good time was my idea of fun, not gardening.'

'And I ruined it by marrying you,' he said quietly, ruefully. 'We had no money to go out.'

She took a sip of her champagne. 'It wasn't entirely your fault. I walked into it with my eyes open.'

'Neither of us saw the pitfalls.'

'We didn't listen to our parents.'

'Are there any kids who do listen when they reach that age?' he wanted to know. 'But the truth is, Ellie, I'd do it all over again.'

She shot a startled look at him, a hunted look, he thought.

'It's true,' he said. 'Unlike you, I never found anyone else to love.'

'What are you saying?' she whispered, and he noticed that her fingers had tightened around the stem of the glass.

He threw caution to the winds. 'That I still love you. That I want us to make a life together again. I want us to have children. I want us to be a family, Ellie. It is all I have ever dreamt about.'

CHAPTER FOUR

THE sound of shattering glass snapped Danielle out of her state of suspended shock, and when she looked down it was to see blood on her fingers and shards of glass on the path at her feet. But she felt no pain and was too numb to move.

She prayed that she hadn't heard Byron correctly. He didn't still love her—he couldn't, it wasn't possible, she didn't want him to. It was the last thing in the world she wanted.

Byron sprang into action. 'Ellie, what have you done?' Whipping a handkerchief out of his pocket, he wrapped it loosely about her hand and led her indoors.

In the kitchen he cleansed her wounds, made sure there were no splinters of glass left, then wrapped the offending fingers with sticking plaster. Not until he was entirely satisfied did he usher her into the lounge and sit her down. 'Now,' he said, 'would you mind telling me what all that was about?'

Neither of them had spoken until this moment, except when he'd asked where she kept her first aid kit. Danielle had been afraid to speak in case she gave herself away, but she had known that questions would follow. The problem was, what did she say?

He had told her that he loved her and she had looked at him as though he had two heads and crumbled her champagne flute in her hand! What sort of a reaction was that, for heaven's sake?

'You shocked me,' she said quietly, eventually, knowing full well that it was no answer but it was the best she could manage.

Dark brows lifted. 'You're saying that you don't believe I'm still in love with you?'

She believed it, all right; the truth was she didn't want it to be true. It would cause too many problems. More than ever she wished Tony were here. She needed a man to protect her from Byron. 'Ten years is a long time,' she pointed out. 'People change.'

Grey eyes narrowed and turned to glittering silver; there was a sudden raw edge to his voice. 'Nine years and seven months, to be precise. And you're the one who's changed, not me.'

She tried to meet his eyes but couldn't, let them rest instead on her injured hand.

'What you're really saying,' he grated, 'is that what you felt for me wasn't true love. Is that right?'

Danielle nodded, unable to put the lie into words.

'And that you don't want me back in your life?'

Again she inclined her head.

'I suppose I should have guessed that when I heard you'd married John Smith,' he snorted in sudden anger. 'Hell, I should have read the warning signs when—' His words were cut off as the doorbell rang. He frowned. 'Are you expecting anyone?'

'No.' But she welcomed the intrusion. Anything that ended this difficult conversation was welcome. Except that when she opened the door she was suddenly not so sure.

'Mother! What are you doing here?'

'Now, what sort of a welcome is that?' asked Evelyn Taylor-Garnham as she sailed into the house. 'If you must know I came to return the earring you lost the other day. I found it under a cushion.'

'Oh, I see. Thank you, Mother.' It was unlike her parent to be so thoughtful. It would have been more in keeping had she phoned and suggested that Danielle collect the gold stud. But what troubled Danielle most at this moment was the any-second-now meeting between Byron and her mother. Perhaps she ought to warn her...

It was already too late. Danielle, tailing behind her parent, saw Byron appear in front of them. His hand was outstretched, his biggest, broadest smile fixed firmly on his lips. 'Evelyn, how nice to see you again after all these years.'

Danielle could not see her face but guessed it would be as black as a thundercloud and ten times as angry. Byron's hand was ignored. 'You!' the older woman exclaimed loudly and furiously. 'What are you doing here?' She was unaware that she had reiterated her own daughter's words of a week before.

'I'm visiting Danielle,' he announced calmly, his eyes filled with mocking amusement.

'I can see that, but the question is why?' insisted the older woman. 'You are no longer a part of her life.' A bright yellow suit covered her more than ample figure and her grey hair was piled high and tinted purple. Danielle had long since given up trying to persuade her mother to dress less outrageously and more in keeping with her age.

'There's no law that says I cannot visit my ex-wife,' Byron said evenly, his eyes flickering towards Danielle as he spoke, as if asking her what direction his answer should take. 'I happened to be in the area and—'

'And I'm sure she was about to throw you out,' finished Evelyn Taylor-Garnham imperiously. 'Or if she wasn't, then she should have been. You have no right to force yourself on her like this.'

Byron looked at Danielle, a smile lurking at the corners of his mouth. 'Have I used force?'

Danielle shook her head. 'I think, Mother, that I should be the judge of whom I invite into my home.'

'So you invited him in, did you?' jeered the woman. 'How could you, Danielle? After all that you've gone through because of this man.'

Afraid that her mother might say too much, Danielle was wondering how she could defuse the situation when Byron said calmly, 'I think we're both well aware of the upset our divorce caused, Evelyn, but that was a long time ago. I am quite sure that Danielle and I are grown-up enough now not to harbour any resentment. In fact I see no reason why we shouldn't be good friends.'

Danielle had been beginning to applaud him until this last sentence. Now she silently screamed. And because she knew her mother wouldn't hesitate to retaliate, and because her mother was not always the most tactful of people, she spoke quickly.

'Weren't you about to go, Byron?' She knew it was no good trying to get rid of her mother; her parent would not set a foot outside the door until Byron had gone.

'Was I?' An eyebrow quirked questioningly.

'I believe so,' she answered, keeping her eyes steady on his, willing him to take the hint and leave. She was terrified of what her mother might say.

For a moment she thought he was going to dig his heels in, but finally he nodded. 'You're right.' He gave her mother another of his wide, designed-to-disarm smiles. 'It was nice meeting you once more. You're looking well. Perhaps we shall have the pleasure again?'

'I distinctly hope not,' the woman retorted coldly. 'I cannot tell you how shocked I am that you've turned up like this. I hope to goodness my daughter has the good sense to ban you from this house in future.'

Danielle saw a taut muscle jerk in Byron's jaw, saw the way his eyes hardened, but he nevertheless kept his smile in place. 'That is entirely up to her. Goodbye, Evelyn.'

Accompanying him to the door, Danielle said softly, 'I'm sorry about my mother.'

'Don't worry,' he said. 'I'm used to it. I'll see you around.' He spoke casually, as though his declaration of love had never been made.

For a moment, after she closed the door behind him, Danielle stood and took a few calming breaths. In one way her mother had come at exactly the right moment—it had put an end to an extremely uncomfortable conversation. But in another her visit was most inopportune. There would be endless questions now, and cautions, and opinions, and advice. And she would have to sit and listen to them all.

In her absence her mother had wandered outside and found the remains of the champagne and strawberry feast. 'What is this?' Evelyn asked sharply when her daughter reappeared.

'We had supper,' announced Danielle, trying to keep her tone light. The topic of Byron Meredith had never been a happy one and it would be easy to turn the conversation into a full-scale argument.

'You *entertained* him?' her mother queried, her pale blue eyes wide with indignation.

'I saw nothing wrong in it.'

'That man!'

'That man was once my husband. I loved him.' And I think I still do, she added silently.

'You need your head examined, Danielle. He is nothing but trouble. What is he doing here? I sincerely hope you're not going to see him again. And just look at that broken glass on the path—and your finger. Did you have an argument?'

Her mother went on and on, as Danielle had known she would, but she let the words sail over her head, not really listening, unable to understand why her parent was still so much against Byron. He was no longer a penniless student but affluent and successful, the sort of man her mother would, under different circumstances, encourage her to go out with.

'I've been invited to a dinner party on Sunday, Danielle, and I've been asked to bring you along too.'

Her heart sank. More of her mother's matchmaking efforts. Since she had refused to marry Tony, her mother had made every effort to find some other man for her.

'Whose party?' she asked. Not that she intended going. She'd attended too many, knew the drill too well. Her mother would gushingly introduce her to the bachelor in question, run through a list of Danielle's good points, and then leave them alone.

'Rod Maston's.'

'Rod?' echoed Danielle. The man who had stepped into John's shoes!

She had considered selling JBS when John died but knew he wouldn't have wanted that; he wouldn't have wanted strangers running the company he had built up from scratch. Rod had been the perfect person for the job. He had been John's right-hand man for so many years that he had taken over with scarcely a hitch. She was on the board, but all the decision-making was left to Rod and the other directors.

She wasn't aware that her mother knew him. He was much older than John, and a nice enough man—a widower also. Surely her mother wasn't thinking of pairing her with him? It was ludicrous. There had to be a twenty-year age gap.

'That's right—Rod.' Her mother smiled mysteriously. 'I thought it would surprise you. It seems he's short of a lady.'

'You say he specifically invited me?'

Evelyn nodded.

In that case she would have to go. She liked Rod but theirs was a strictly business relationship, and she fervently hoped that his invitation was genuine, not something her mother had organised.

Danielle spent three sleepless nights worrying about Byron's declaration of love and the implications it brought, and it took a great deal of effort to push him out of her mind on Sunday evening. She had decided that come what may she was going to enjoy herself.

The day had been hot with clear blue skies but now it had begun to cloud over. The forecast was that they were going to pay for the recent spell of hot weather with thunderstorms, although they weren't due until the early hours of the morning. She would be home and tucked up in bed by then.

She and her mother shared a taxi and, never having been to Rod's house before, Danielle was pleasantly impressed. It looked as though it was several cottages knocked into one, with white rendered walls, lots of chimneys, and tiny square paned windows. It faced the village green and behind it was a small area of woodland. It looked enchanting.

Rod himself greeted them at the door, smart in navy blazer and flannels, his still thick grey hair immaculately combed. 'I'm glad you could make it,' he said to

Danielle, taking her hand and kissing her politely on the cheek. 'You've rescued the day. I do so hate odd numbers.'

But the kiss he gave her mother was far from perfunctory, and Danielle watched in total amazement as they hugged. What *was* going on?

They both turned to look at her, happy smiles lighting their faces. 'We thought you should know,' said Rod.

Evelyn nodded, seeming for once at a loss for words.

'It's quite a shock,' admitted Danielle.

'But a nice one, I hope?' Rod suggested.

Her mother slipped her hand into Rod's and looked up into his face. 'We're very happy.'

'Then I'm pleased for you,' Danielle said. She had always hoped that her mother would find herself another man; Evelyn was not the type to live the rest of her life alone.

Inside, guests were talking and sipping pre-dinner drinks, and Rod began his introductions. Some people Danielle already knew as they were employees of JBS but others were strangers. They worked their way slowly around the room until they were back where they'd started.

Sally James and her sales manager husband David had been joined by a tall, dark-haired man. He had his back to them but there was no disguising his breadth of shoulder or the arrogant tilt of his head.

A lump lodged in Danielle's throat. She hoped and prayed it wasn't Byron, but she knew that it was, and she wondered if he was the odd man—the reason she had been invited!

Her mother had not yet realised who he was, but the moment he turned Danielle heard her gasp of dismay.

'Evelyn, Danielle,' said Rod, 'I'd like you to meet the eminent architect, Byron Meredith.'

Byron's momentary shock was hidden superbly behind a smile and Danielle wondered whether she was the only person to have seen it.

'Byron—' Rod continued his introductions '—this is my very good friend, Evelyn Taylor-Garnham, and her lovely daughter Danielle. Danielle is John Smith's wife. You remember him?'

Byron nodded. 'We actually already know each other.' He took Danielle's hand into his big warm one, squeezing it gently, his eyes never leaving her face.

'You met when you were working on the gallery project?' assumed Rod with a frown.

'Long before that,' Byron informed him easily. 'Danielle was still at school as a matter of fact.'

'Goodness,' said Rod. 'I had no idea. What a small world it is.'

At Rod's side Evelyn glowered and walked away. Rod frowned and hurried after her, Sally and David began to speak to someone else, and Danielle was left alone with the man who was forbidden to her for ever.

'This really is a most welcome surprise.' Byron couldn't believe his good fortune. He'd not been looking forward to this evening, couldn't think why he had accepted Rod's invitation, except that he had hoped it would help take his mind off Danielle.

After he'd left her house he had forced himself to believe that he would never see her again. She had made it crystal-clear that there was no place for him in her life, that her feelings for him were zero, that her love for him was no more—if it had ever been there in the first place!

It had been hard for him to accept that she wanted nothing more to do with him—in fact he could not; he refused to; he felt sure there must be some way to win her back. And now the opportunity had been given to him. It was the most incredible piece of good luck.

He took her other hand and closed the space between them. His adorable Ellie, perfect in oyster silk, smelling like a dream, looking like an angel. His hormones played havoc and he desperately wanted to whisk her away to somewhere they could make wild and exhilarating love.

'I wasn't aware that you knew Rod well enough to be invited to his home,' said Danielle in a quiet, tight little voice.

He knew that she wanted to pull away, that she wanted to be anywhere except here at his side, but he had no intention of letting her go. Fate had delivered her into his hands and he was determined to play it for all it was worth.

'Actually I don't,' he told her. 'We've met purely on a business level, but when he invited me along this evening I thought, Why not?' And was he glad now that he had accepted!

'He felt sorry for you because you're living in a hotel, is that it?' she questioned sharply, making it clear that she did not.

'I'd actually been wondering whether I dared come and see you again,' he admitted. 'Except that after my visit on Thursday I gained the impression that I wouldn't be welcome. Is that so?'

'You know very well it is,' she answered fiercely. 'I don't want you in my life, ever.'

The words pierced his heart with the swiftness of an arrow. 'You don't even want to be friends? Did I hurt you that much?' It was hard to accept. Impossible, in fact. He had always held onto the belief that one day...

'It's not a matter of whether you hurt me or not, Byron. We've grown apart—can't you see that? You have your life; I have mine.'

'And you don't think the two should meet?'

Danielle shook her head. 'Frankly, no.'

'You don't have much of a life,' he said softly. And still he held her hands. He never, ever wanted to let her go.

'I'm happy,' she said.

'So you keep saying, but I'm sure I could make you happier. No woman as beautiful as you should live alone.'

He thought back to when they had married, when they'd moved into their little terraced house in the Birmingham suburbs and had been as happy as any two people could be. They had each promised to love one other for ever. She hadn't been lying to him then, he was sure.

Right from their first meeting there had been an invisible cord drawing one to the other, as though fate had decreed they should meet and fall in love and get married and spend the rest of their lives together.

So what had gone wrong? Why did she love him no more? He still loved her, desperately. It had been pushed into the back of his mind while she'd been married to John, but now it had been fuelled back into life and was in danger of exploding.

He lifted her hands and kissed each of her fingers in turn, and then Evelyn Taylor-Garnham's strident tones sliced into the air between them. 'Danielle! Dinner is about to be served.'

Byron came back to the present with a start, as though

he had been snapped out of a hypnotic trance, and he felt Danielle jump too. And they both realised that almost everyone had filed through to the dining room.

'We could make a smart exit,' he whispered in her ear.

'You wouldn't dare!' Danielle's blue eyes were wide.

And incredibly beautiful, he thought. 'Wouldn't I? Just say the word and we'll leave right this minute.'

But she didn't, of course. She followed her mother and he walked at her side. Evelyn sat down beside Rod and Byron and Danielle took the only two places left at the other end of the long table. Altogether there were a dozen people, and it suited Byron that he and Danielle were sitting together, though he sensed that she would have preferred otherwise.

Throughout the meal Evelyn's eyes were upon them and it wasn't difficult to imagine what she was thinking. He would have bet his last pound that had she known he was going to be present she would have persuaded her daughter not to come. She must be seething inside. In fact if looks could kill he would be stone-cold dead by now.

Conversation was general, the whole table joining in, and afterwards they had coffee in the lounge. The French windows were thrown wide because it was still very warm, despite the promised rain, and he saw Danielle slip outside. But before he could follow Rod put a hand on his shoulder.

'Why did you never say that you were once married to Danielle? You could have knocked me down with a feather when Eve told me. Danielle never said anything about being married before either. I truly thought John was her first husband.'

'We were only kids,' said Byron with a shrug, trying

to make light of it. 'Too young to know our own minds.' Which wasn't strictly true, at least not as far as he was concerned, but it was as much as he was saying.

'It's incredible.' Rod shook his head as if still trying to come to terms with it. 'And such a pity about John. He was a good man.'

'Yes, I heard about the accident,' said Byron.

'If you could call it that,' commented Rod drily.

Byron frowned. 'What do you mean? Are you suggesting that it wasn't an accident?'

But before he could answer Evelyn caught hold of Rod's arm and dragged him away. She did not even look at Byron.

Byron thought about Rod's cryptic comment as he made his way out into the garden. If John's death hadn't been an accident, then what was he implying? For Danielle's sake he did not like the sound of it, and it was definitely something he intended taking up with Rod the next time they spoke. Meanwhile he had other things on his mind...

The garden had rambling paths and hidden corners and it took him a few minutes to find Danielle. She sat in a rose arbour and appeared deep in thought. Yellow climbing roses spilled their heavy scent into the air and his footsteps were muffled by the camomile path. He stood a few moments, looking at her.

She was so beautiful. He had been the world's biggest fool ever to let her go. The trouble was he had been too immature in those days, lacking in confidence. He should have made more of an effort, though. If he'd been firm and got past her mother then none of this would have happened. They'd never have got divorced, she wouldn't have remarried, they would have sorted themselves out and still been together. They would have had three or four children by now as well. More than anything he wanted children. Ellie's children.

'Ellie.' He spoke quietly, and she was startled to see him. 'I wondered where you'd got to.'

'Can't a girl have any privacy?' She looked angry that he had followed her. 'Why do you think I came out here?'

It hurt to think that it had been to avoid him but he made no attempt to go away. Instead he sat down beside her, and her perfume mingled with that of the roses. It was like an instant aphrodisiac.

'I don't know why you keep pestering me,' she muttered fiercely.

'I wasn't aware that was what I'm doing.'

'You keep turning up. That's enough. How often do I have to tell you that I want you out of my life?'

The arrowhead turned viciously in his heart. 'I don't think that's going to be possible, Ellie. Even if I have to start all over again, I'm going to make you fall back in love with me.' He took her hand and pressed it against his heart. 'Can you feel that? Can you feel how strongly it beats? It's yours. It always has been and always will be.'

The moment he uttered the words he knew he had made yet another mistake. The last thing he wanted was to drive her away altogether.

Even now she jumped to her feet and looked down at him with eyes full of hatred. 'Keep away from me, Byron Meredith. Do you hear? Keep away!' And with that she ran back towards the house.

Raindrops began to fall.

CHAPTER FIVE

DANIELLE'S only thought was to go home, to put as much space between her and Byron as possible. She wished now that she had come in her own car rather than by taxi. It was not going to be easy to escape before Byron found her.

Sitting close to him on the bench, touching him, feeling his heartbeat, had sent her pulses racing and her heart totally crazy. It was something he must never find out; he must never know how vulnerable she was.

She wanted to free the love she felt for him more than anything in the world, but she could not, dared not, must never, ever let herself get close to him. The knowledge that he could never have children by her would tear him apart.

It made her think back to when the news had been broken, what it had done to her. She had been completely destroyed for many long months, had wanted to speak to no one, see no one, do nothing but shut herself away. She had felt less than whole, imperfect, unlovable—and that was how Byron would see her if he ever found out.

She felt the beginnings of a headache—she'd had many migraines in those long black days. Fresh air would do her good; she would walk home rather than call a taxi. It was but a few miles.

There was no sign of Byron yet, and Rod and her mother were deep in conversation, so very quietly she slipped out of the house. Maybe she should have told someone, but every second counted.

At first she did not feel the rain, was not even aware of it, her mind totally consumed by the man she was running away from, the man she loved, the man who declared he loved her. Please, God, make him keep away from me, she prayed. I don't think I'm strong enough for this.

It was not until she heard the rumble of thunder that it occurred to her that it was raining—and she was wet—and she still had another two miles to go! She quickened her steps, her head bent against the now driving rain, and she shivered.

Her dress was plastered to her body, her feet squelched in her thin sandals, and she wished belatedly that she hadn't decided to walk. But there was no turning back. She'd have a shower when she got in and go to bed with a hot, milky drink. A little rain hurt no one.

But it was not a little. It came down in torrents, and the thunder was getting nearer, and the flashes of lightning jagged through the sky as though they were searching for her.

She was not afraid of storms, but she definitely wasn't happy about being outdoors in the middle of one. There wasn't even any shelter, except for trees, and she intended to avoid those like the plague. She remembered a schoolfriend who had got struck by lightning under a tree. She hadn't been seriously hurt, but badly enough for Danielle not to take the risk.

The heavy skies had brought about a premature nightfall, and she realised now the foolishness of attempting to walk home. A fast-moving car sent a shower of muddy water over her. She shook her fist and soldiered on. It was a fairly quiet lane so there wasn't much traffic, but when the next car came she stepped back into the hedge to avoid a further deluge.

When the car slowed down she silently thanked the driver's courtesy, but then it stopped altogether and the passenger door opened. Byron's savage voice ordered her in.

Grateful and dismayed at the same time, she flung herself onto his leather upholstery, hoping she did not ruin it. He was the last person she wanted a lift from, and yet she hadn't been looking forward to trudging yet another mile in this horrendous weather.

The storm was right overhead now, and lightning struck a tree less than a hundred yards in front of them. Danielle gave a cry of real fear as the tree split in two and one half came crashing across the lane.

If Byron hadn't turned up, if he hadn't stopped and forced her to stop too, she would have been right under that tree now. Possibly dead, or at the very least seriously injured.

'Have you taken leave of your senses, Danielle?' He pushed a clean handkerchief into her hand so that she could mop her streaming face.

She had never seen him so angry. His eyes were as silver as the lightning that fizzed and crackled around them, his brow as dark as the thunderclouds above, his mouth grim.

'What the devil possessed you to try and walk home in this weather?' he wanted to know.

'How did I know it was going to rain?' she flung back.

'Because it had already started when we were out in the garden. Am I so abhorrent to you that you'd risk your life to get away from me?'

Danielle closed her eyes, wrapping her arms around herself as she began to shiver uncontrollably.

'Drink this.'

The harsh command snapped her eyes open and a leather-covered flask was pushed into her hand. The smell of brandy almost made her gag. She hated the stuff, but obediently she put it to her lips and took a tiny sip.

'More,' he grated.

Another sip.

'And again.'

She swallowed a whole mouthful this time, and immediately it began to warm her.

Byron screwed the top back on and then barked another request. 'Take your dress off.'

'I beg your pardon?' She blinked at him.

'I said take it off. The way you're shivering, you'll catch pneumonia. You can wear my jacket.' He shrugged out of it even as he spoke.

Danielle knew what he said made sense, but even so...

'Do I have to do it for you?'

With trembling hands she slid the destroyed silk from her shoulders, wriggled it down over her hips and let it slide into a sodden heap at her feet. She was too miserable to feel embarrassed.

He handed her his jacket and she struggled her way into it, which was difficult when she was so wet. She wrapped it around her, and coupled with the brandy it soon began to make her feel better.

The car was still where he had stopped it but he kept the engine running and the heater turned high. There was no going forward because of the tree that blocked the road, and not enough room to turn around.

The windows were misted and the storm still raged, but there were no trees near enough to pose a further threat. Danielle knew they were safe in the car—as safe as she ever could be in Byron's presence!

'Now answer this question,' he grated. 'Do you really hate me so much that you cannot bear to touch me?'

She didn't answer—she couldn't—saying instead, 'I think you'd be doing both of us a favour if you kept away.'

'Tonight was not planned,' he pointed out.

'Maybe not,' she agreed with a shrug. 'But you didn't have to monopolise me. You didn't have to follow me out into the garden.'

'No, I didn't have to, but I wanted to.' He was half-turned in his seat towards her, and his eyes were no longer silver but a clear grey and intent on her face. The harshness had gone and he looked relaxed enough to sit and talk for as long as the storm raged.

'I could not believe my good fortune when I saw you,' he said. 'It was like a prayer being answered. I had no idea I'd ever see you again—and suddenly there you were. How I stopped myself from kissing you I don't know.'

'I'm glad you did,' she retorted tersely, 'because I'd have slapped your face and you might have found that rather embarrassing.'

'Would you slap me if I kissed you now?' He leaned closer towards her.

Danielle felt her heart go into panic but she made herself sit still and show none of her fear. She lifted her chin aggressively instead. 'Without a doubt. Although I somehow don't think you'd take advantage; you'd never force yourself on me.'

Byron nodded. 'I agree that it's something I've never done, but I've never felt like this before either. I've never wanted anyone as much as I want you at this moment, Ellie.'

He wanted more than a kiss! Was that what he was saying? She closed her eyes and it was her undoing, because she felt his breath warm and fresh on her cheek, and the next instant his mouth captured hers.

It was not a demanding kiss; it was gentle and questioning and he was ready to withdraw if she raised an objection. But she didn't; she couldn't. She was shocked into submission, shocked by her own strength of feeling.

She had fought her love for him, had thought she would be able to hold him at bay. She had not expected this instant flare of passion that, if she didn't hurry and do something about it, would tell him without words how she felt.

But for some reason she did not move. She allowed the kiss; she let him deepen it. Fire burned in her belly, and although she did not actually respond neither did she fight him. And before she could stop it a faint moan of desire escaped her throat.

He crushed her then; his hands slid inside the jacket and found the soft warmth of her skin. His mouth made urgent demands and she kissed him back with a hunger that frightened her.

Byron slipped the jacket from her shoulders and his burning lips trailed slowly and achingly down the arch of her throat, finding the rapidly beating pulse at its base and the damp, softly rounded curve of her breast.

Danielle was completely within his power. She threaded her fingers through the thick blackness of his hair, luxuriating in the familiar shape of his head, the familiar male scent of his body, and she asked herself why she had ever walked out on him.

'Ellie. Ellie.' He muttered her name over and over

again and, before she knew it, his mouth was on her breasts, sucking first one hardened nipple and then the other into it as though he were a starving man in need of sustenance.

It was sweet, sweet torture and a well of longing rose up inside her. Her head had long since lolled back on the seat, her lips were parted, her eyes closed, and she was in a world of exquisite pleasure. Every single promise she had made to herself flew out of the window—until a particularly vivid flash of lightning, which she could see even through her eyelids, coupled with a roll of thunder immediately overhead, brought her to her senses with a jolt.

She pushed Byron away, her blue eyes creating their own sparks of lightning. 'You should not have done that, Byron Meredith.' She did not stop to think that she had been equally guilty.

'It's what I've dreamt of night after night,' he muttered thickly, emotionally. 'You taste so good, Ellie, far, far better than I remember. You've become a woman, an extremely exciting woman, a sensual woman. And, Lord help me, I want you.'

With a further flash of her turbulent blue eyes Danielle dragged his jacket back around her, holding it tight at the throat, hiding her aching breasts from his greedy eyes, trying also to hide her own pain of exquisite pleasure. 'Don't waste time hoping,' she thrust fiercely. 'This is the first and last time you're going to touch me.'

Smouldering eyes narrowed. 'You mean you're going to continue the cold shoulder treatment?' His voice was gruff—not with pleasure now but the beginning of anger.

Danielle nodded. 'That's exactly right.'

'So why did you let me kiss you?'

She shrugged. 'I guess I was curious.'

'Curious?' He shot out the word explosively. 'About what, for heaven's sake?'

'About how I felt.'

'And?' There was a stillness about him, a sudden hard glitter in his eyes.

'It proved any feelings I had for you are long since dead.' She hated lying but it had to be done.

Byron's eyes narrowed suspiciously. 'Am I supposed to believe that?'

'You can believe what you like,' she retorted crisply, 'but it happens to be true.'

To her amazement he smiled. The anger went as suddenly as it had appeared. 'You were never a good liar, Ellie, sweetheart. You enjoyed that kiss equally as much as I did. Deny it if you dare.'

She shrugged, hiding her alarm. 'Maybe I did,' she answered coolly. 'But I'm not interested in an affair, and that's all it would be. It wouldn't mean anything.'

He studied her face long and hard, and it was difficult not to look away. Somehow, though, she managed it, and when he finally sank back into his seat and faced the front she gave a silent sigh of relief.

He gripped the steering wheel with both hands and the tension in him was tangible. The storm continued to rumble around them, though it was moving away, and the rain no longer drummed on the roof of the car.

Another few minutes, thought Danielle, and we'll be able to move.

'I think we ought to tell your mother that you're safe,' he said, reaching for his car phone and dialling a number.

Danielle frowned. 'She knows you came after me?'

'Rod saw you slip out of the house, but neither of them realised you were going home. I'm afraid I invented the excuse that you had a headache and had gone for a walk. When the heavens opened, I said I'd come and pick you up. They're expecting you back.'

'Looking like this?' shrieked Danielle. 'Wild horses wouldn't drag me there.'

'You look beautiful.'

'You're crazy.' Or blind.

'I love you.'

She closed her eyes to hide the torment in her soul. 'I want to go home.' But she did not want Byron to take her. 'I think the storm's passing; I should be able to make it now.'

'Are you forgetting the tree?'

'I can climb over it.'

'There's still over a mile to go. You're being ridiculous, Ellie.' And then his call was finally answered. 'Oh, hello, Rod. Yes. Yes, I have her with me, looking a little like a drowned rat. I'm taking her home. Tell Evelyn, will you? And thanks for a lovely meal. Danielle says the same. Yes, I'll be seeing you. *Ciao.*'

'So that's settled,' he said as he put the phone back down.

To his satisfaction, but not hers. 'What are you going to do? Shift the tree single-handedly?' she demanded scathingly.

He grinned. 'There's an opening back there I can reverse into. Do not worry, my sweet, I'll get you home safe and sound.'

And then he would invite himself in, and it was not difficult to guess what would happen next.

Byron turned on the demister, and as soon as he could see where he was going he reversed the car down the lane. Five minutes later he pulled up outside her house.

'A hot shower for you, young lady,' he said firmly as he took the keys from her and unlocked the door.

Danielle shook her head. 'I must check on the horses.'

But first she had to get dressed. Byron's jacket had been all right in the car, but when she stood up she was barely decent.

She ran upstairs and pulled on a pair of jeans and a sweater, and ran back down where she slid her feet into wellingtons and grabbed a waterproof on her way out. She did not even notice Byron following, picking his way through the muddy paddock in his Italian leather shoes.

Sandor and Morgan were huddled together in one of the stables, pawing the ground, eyes rolling, ears flattened back. Danielle approached them cautiously, talking softly and reassuringly all the time.

Thankfully the storm had moved away—even the rain had almost stopped—and eventually the horses became less tense. She could feel their bodies relaxing as she continued to talk to them and stroke them and kiss them, but it was a long time before she felt that she could happily leave them.

It was then that she saw Byron. He was standing just inside the doorway watching her. 'I wish I was a horse,' he said quietly.

Danielle did not answer. Loving animals, she decided, was far safer than loving human beings. They made no demands, they were totally loyal, and they never broke your heart.

They trudged back to the house, Danielle in her sensible green wellingtons, Byron in his shirtsleeves and fine leather shoes. Not that he complained, or even seemed to notice.

On the horizon she noticed a break in the clouds where the sky glowed red from a summer sun that had not long set. Soon it would be clear again, and the only storm that would rage would be the one in her heart.

Indoors Byron once again ordered her to take a much

needed shower, but it was not until she looked at herself in the bathroom mirror that Danielle realised what a complete mess she was. Her hair hung in rat's tails and her mascara ran in streaks down her face.

She looked truly awful and yet Byron had kissed her and told her that she was beautiful and that he loved her! Tears sprang to her eyes at the futility of it all and blindly she turned on the shower.

For several minutes she stood beneath its dousing jets without moving; she simply let it rain down over her as if by doing so it would wash away all her problems.

She kept her eyes closed and did not hear the bathroom door open, or Byron stripping off his own wet clothes; she was not even aware of the shower door opening. The first she knew of Byron's presence was when his firm male body brushed against hers. Her eyes snapped wide open and she cried out in alarm.

Byron knew the risk he was taking but he felt that it was worth it. 'I thought I'd save water,' he said with a grin.

Danielle's reaction was as he had expected—furious. 'I bet you did,' she cried. 'If you want a shower then go back to your hotel and have one.' And she shrank back against the wall.

'You don't mean that?' He was happy with the knowledge that he was no longer up against an insurmountable barrier. Her response in the car had been like the sun coming out from behind a particularly large cloud, and he was much more confident now in his pursuit of her.

Her eyes had turned an incredible, almost luminous blue, like a tropical ocean in which he could bask. He wondered if she had any idea how beautiful they were when she was angry.

'Oh, yes, I do mean it,' she insisted. 'Don't you realise the liberty you're taking?'

He did, very much so, but he was hoping to get away with it. He wanted to look at her, all of her, every inch of her exciting naked body, and it was difficult to keep his eyes on her face, but he knew that for the moment he must.

'This is something I've always wanted to do,' he murmured. 'I know we used to bathe together, and that was fantastic, but showering is something completely different, don't you agree?'

They'd had no shower in their little terraced house but it had been a ritual for them to share a bath. Ten years ago he had thought it was the ultimate in eroticism but he could think of a thousand different ways to stimulate desire now.

'It's also very personal.' Danielle crossed her arms over her chest and glared. 'If you're so badly in need of a shower, then *I'll* get out.'

She made to move but he put his hands on the wall on either side of her shoulders, careful not to touch her, but close enough for desire to sizzle from one to the other. He could almost smell her arousal and was fairly sure that only fear of giving herself away made her protest.

'Byron, let me go.'

He smiled and allowed his fingers to touch her face, to touch the dozens of tiny freckles he so adored, to trace the outline of her jaw, to stroke across her eyelids and her fantastic mouth. 'I can't do that, Ellie,' he whispered hoarsely, and felt the tremor that ran through her.

Gently he removed her hands from her breasts, holding her eyes with his as he did so, and then he proceeded to squeeze a liberal amount of shower gel into his palm.

Knowing what was coming, Danielle closed her eyes and gave herself up to the inevitable.

He took his time, soaping her from the top of each arm to the tips of each finger, then over her breasts, careful not to give them any more attention than anywhere else, even though he was aching to do so. She felt so good, so much better than he remembered. Now her back and her hips and stomach, now her very secret places. Oh, Lord, how could he control himself when his manhood was completely misbehaving?

When he had finished, amazing even himself with his iron self-control, he said quietly, 'It's your turn now.' And when she did not speak, when she remained standing there with her eyes closed, he took her hands and made her cup them. Then he squeezed gel into them.

'Now wash me,' he ordered, and held his breath.

Her touch was almost his undoing. Had he not instilled into himself that he must take things slowly, he would have made love to her there and then. She was as thorough as he had been, the only difference being that he had his eyes open.

He loved watching her, seeing the struggle she had with her emotions. When she reached the most male part of him she hesitated for only a moment before taking him into her palm.

But her touch, the soft stroke of her fingers, was his downfall. His control snapped. With an anguished cry his arms snaked out to clasp her hips and pull her hard against him. He had to make love to her here and now; he could wait no longer…

CHAPTER SIX

DANIELLE found Byron in the kitchen wearing only his black underpants. His shirt, socks and trousers were in the tumble-drier, his muddy shoes by the back door. Two mugs of drinking chocolate steamed on the worktop.

'I was just about to come and fetch you,' he said. 'What took you so long?'

His near-nudity appeared not to concern him, and it shouldn't have concerned her either, but it did. She couldn't keep her eyes off him. He had used to be so skinny and pale, now he was lightly tanned and powerfully muscled, vitally masculine in every way. Just looking at him took her breath away. 'I wasn't aware that there was any hurry,' she answered huskily.

'I've made you a drink,' he said. 'And as soon as my clothes are dry I'll be on my way.' There was no sign now of the passion that had racked him earlier.

Danielle had been stunned beyond belief when he'd suddenly opened the shower door and leapt out, muttering something about being out of his mind, and instead of thanking her lucky stars for her narrow escape she had been hugely disappointed.

His hands on her body, touching him too—no, more than touching, *caressing,* feeling the exciting hardness of him—had aroused her so totally that letting Byron make love to her had seemed the most natural thing in the world. She wouldn't have stopped him; she couldn't have done. Even now her body was still sensitised, still attuned to him, still wanting him.

So why had he backed off?

She had asked herself this question a dozen times over as she'd towelled herself dry, and she was asking it again now. Had he perhaps been testing her? Had she given him his answer? Would his pursuit of her be relentless now that he knew how easy it was to get past her defences?

Thinking about it logically, she'd had a lucky escape. In future she would need to be doubly on her guard, insist at all times that she felt nothing for him. Any lapses would have to be put down to pure physical desire, nothing more. Certainly not love. She closed her eyes for a second. Why did life have to be so painful?

Picking up her mug of chocolate, she slipped onto one of the stools at the breakfast bar. Byron joined her, and the musky male smell of him was almost her undoing. She wanted to be held by him, she wanted to kiss him, she wanted...

'Why do you think your mother never told Rod that you'd been married before?'

Thank goodness for a safe topic of conversation. She lifted her shoulders and pulled a wry face. 'She tells no one; she prefers to forget it.'

'Forget me, you mean,' he said tersely. 'I was never her favourite person. How long has she been seeing Rod?'

Again Danielle gave a half-shrug. 'I've no idea. It was a complete surprise when I saw how it was between them. She's never even mentioned him. I've been trying to work out how they met. I imagine that it was at someone's house party; my mother goes to a lot of those. I don't think they've known each other long.'

'Why do you say that?'

'Because it's only recently that she's had this—what

can I call it?—this ethereal look about her. I didn't know what it was; I couldn't put my finger on it. I thought perhaps she was plotting something. Now I know that it is love.'

'Are you pleased for her?'

'Absolutely. It's time she found herself another man. And with someone to occupy her mind maybe it will stop her trying to find a husband for me.'

Byron frowned sharply, stopping his cup halfway to his lips, his eyes questioning on hers. 'She does that often?'

'It's what I thought tonight was about. I think she was as dismayed as me when the spare man turned out to be you.'

Her mother had never understood why she had turned down Tony Cochran.

'You're being foolish,' she had chided her daughter. 'You're too young to live alone for the rest of your life, and you're not going to get marriage offers for ever.'

Maybe she was foolish, thought Danielle wearily. Tony had said that he didn't mind that she couldn't have children, but Danielle minded; she minded very much. Tony was an only child, and his parents were dead too. She felt quite sure that he must want children of his own, no matter what he said. In time he would have held it against her.

A muscle jerked in Byron's jaw, his eyes now narrowed with suspicion. 'Are you seeing any of these men?'

'Would it bother you if I was?'

'Of course it damn well would,' he snarled.

Danielle saw the tension in his hands as they cradled the mug. 'Well, it shouldn't,' she said firmly. 'I don't have to answer to you any more, Byron.' She picked up her own white mug with its yellow sunflower design and took a sip of the dark, rich liquid. It was delicious, and brought back memories of the early days of their marriage when they'd always drunk chocolate before going to bed.

'Is there any particular man in your life at this moment?'

She gave a slow smile. 'No one you need worry about.'

'But there is someone.' Byron dragged in an angry breath. 'I bet he's rich as well. Who is he? Why haven't you told me about him before?'

'I saw no reason to,' she said quietly.

'No reason?' he yelled, suddenly violently angry. 'I think you have every reason. What the hell do you think I'm doing here? Why do you think I've kept coming to see you? If there's no hope then tell me and I'll make myself scarce.'

'Haven't I been trying to do that?' she asked quietly.

Byron closed his eyes, and there was a long moment's silence. Danielle could almost hear his mind working and she could sense his deep disappointment.

When finally he looked at her his eyes were unreadable. 'It must have been a bitter blow when John died.'

A complete change of subject! Why? Painful memories flooded back. 'Naturally. No one ever expects something like that to happen.'

'A most tragic accident,' he agreed.

A sudden lump in her throat made it difficult to swallow. The accident had upset her deeply. 'The saddest part about it is that it could have been avoided if John had been wearing a hard hat. He might have been hurt, but not fatally.'

'So you don't blame anyone?'

She shook her head. 'Not really.'

'Do you plan to marry again?'

'No.'

'Why?'

'Because I don't seem to have much luck where marriage is concerned.'

'So there's no one really serious in your life?'

She smiled wryly. He hadn't changed the conversation at all, merely gone a different way about it. 'Why does it bother you so much?'

'You know damn well why,' he said with a sudden snarl.

'I know you claim to still love me, but I don't believe you. If your love for me was so deep you would never have let me go, you would have done something to save our marriage.'

'Don't you think I haven't regretted that a million times over?' he demanded. 'Your interfering mother stopped me in the first place, as you very well know. But because you'd always said that money was at the root of our problems I finished university and got myself a well-paid job. And then what did I find? That in the meantime you'd married a man with even more of the filthy stuff.'

Danielle grimaced. 'Maybe I was wrong about the money side of things; maybe you and I simply weren't compatible.'

He snorted derisively, his eyes a glittering silver as they locked with hers. 'Do you really believe that?'

A trickle of ice ran down Danielle's spine as she felt the full power of his sexuality. Her stomach crunched and her pulses throbbed and she longed more than anything to launch herself into his arms. It was sheer hell, denying herself this man.

But she lifted her chin firmly. 'I have no doubt about it.' How she managed to say the words she did not know, but she could sit beside him no longer. She finished her drink, jumped down from the stool and rinsed her mug under the tap.

'How can you be so sure?'

He was there behind her, his breath warm on the back of her neck. Danielle froze and prayed he would not touch her again. If he did it would be her undoing.

'Because I know my own mind,' she told him firmly. 'I wouldn't have married again if I'd still had some feelings for you. John meant everything to me.'

'And now there's someone else. I've lost out again. My timing could not have been worse.' He looked and sounded utterly dejected.

The telephone rang into the silence that followed his words. It was Danielle's mother, wanting to know whether Byron was still there.

'Yes, Mother, he is,' she said.

'Tell her I'm just going,' Byron called out.

She saw him move through to the utility room and pluck his shirt from the tumble-drier, and by the time the call was finished he was fully dressed again.

He led the way to the front door, grim-faced and silent. 'Thank you for bringing me home,' said Danielle quietly, achingly.

'It was the least I could do.'

She watched as he walked out to his car. She watched as he drove away. The tears came slowly. She was crying for Byron now, because he loved her, and because there was no future for them together.

'Rod, I assure you the crack is getting wider.' Byron looked urgently into the other man's face. 'And if something isn't done about it soon there are going to be real problems. What the hell are Scotts playing at? You said you would sort it out with them. Don't you realise my good name's at stake here?'

Scotts were the builders who had been contracted by JBS to build the gallery. Byron had even taken matters into his own hands when he'd first spotted the problem and gone to see them himself. But despite several attempts no one was ever available to speak to him.

Rod looked faintly guilty. 'There are complications. Scotts have gone out of business.'

A string of swear words filled the room and Byron bounced to his feet. 'What sort of a two-bit company did you use, for heaven's sake?'

Rod shook his head. 'They've always had a good reputation, I assure you; I've put business their way many times in the past. Their problems seem to have started with a change of management. We're not the only ones to have complaints filed against them.'

'Why the hell didn't you tell me any of this before?' Byron demanded furiously.

Rod raked his fingers through his thick grey hair, worry lines creasing his brow. 'Because I've only just found out myself. It's sent shock waves through the industry.'

'So what's going to happen to the gallery? How about the warranty? Who's going to put things right?' Lord, this was worse than he had thought. He rubbed his hand across the back of his neck as he felt the beginning of a very real headache.

'I'm working on it,' said Rod.

Byron snorted, his eyes a storm-cloud grey. 'And how long is that going to take? Until the building's fallen down? Dammit, man, this is serious.'

Rod spread his hands expansively. 'You think I don't know? You think I'm not as concerned as you?'

'I guess you are,' said Byron with a heavy sigh. 'But it's one hell of a thing to be told.' He sat down again. 'I need a good, strong cup of coffee—preferably laced with whisky.'

'I can manage the coffee,' said Rod, and buzzed through to his secretary.

Byron decided it was time to change the subject, before he blew his top altogether. 'It was a good meal last night, Rod. Thanks for inviting me.'

'I'm glad you could make it.' Rod smiled at last. 'I still can't get over the fact that you and Danielle were once married.'

'It's true enough,' said Byron, but he didn't want to talk about it.

He'd had such high hopes of persuading Danielle to marry him again and he'd been completely gutted when she'd implied last night that there was someone else in her life. He hadn't slept a wink. He couldn't understand why her new boyfriend was never around, why they had never bumped into each other. It was almost as if she had been just saying it to get rid of him.

He mentally shook his head and turned his attention back to Rod. 'What were you saying yesterday about John's accident?'

Surprisingly Rod looked faintly afraid. 'Nothing; I should have kept my mouth shut. Forget it.'

'I can't do that,' said Byron. 'Not where Danielle's concerned. If John's death wasn't a straightforward accident then I want to know about it.'

Rod grimaced uncomfortably. 'Danielle thought the world of John.'

'She need not know about your suspicions.' And he

didn't need it ramming down his throat that Danielle had loved John more than she'd loved him. Nor could he help wondering how much she loved this other guy. She had responded in the shower; he could have taken her easily. Could there be hope? Ought he to try again?

'I never had any actual proof,' said Rod quietly.

'I don't care about proof, I want to know what you think.'

Rod shot a look at the clock on his wall. 'I have to be out of here in five minutes, Byron. Let's talk some other time.'

'When? Tonight over dinner?' Byron felt sure Rod was evading the issue; he looked like a scared little rabbit.

'I can't, I'm going to the theatre. I'll give you a ring, Byron. Now, if you'll excuse me, there's something I need to discuss with my secretary.'

Byron was even more intrigued now, and if Rod was saying nothing then he would take steps to find out for himself. He would hire a private detective if necessary, and for however long it took he would stay right here in Birmingham. For the moment he had no pressing business, nothing that he couldn't handle by telephone or through the computer link-up he'd had installed in his hotel room.

In the first place he'd simply been passing through the city and had been unable to resist taking a look at the gallery. He often did that with buildings he'd designed. The crack—that no one else had apparently spotted— had horrified him, and now this further development meant that he could be here for some while yet.

More time to see Danielle! If she would let him. And there would be no treading softly now. This guy, whoever he was, had to go. Byron intended winning Danielle back no matter what. He would give her a few days' breathing space, and then...

Danielle kept herself busy during the days following Rod's dinner party, riding hard, spending more time at the shop than usual. But even though she was trying not to think about Byron it was predictably impossible. He filled her head every waking moment, and most of her sleeping ones as well.

She desperately hoped that he would make no further attempts to seek her out; she could not handle the pressure. She had been so close to giving herself to him—would have done so if he hadn't backed off—and the more time she spent with him, the harder it would be. One way or another she had to keep him out of her life.

Hopefully, her mention of another man would keep him off her back. She ought to have done it before. She had been giving him hope when there was none.

A whole week passed and she saw nothing of him, a week in which she was both thankful and despairing at the same time.

Her mother had grilled her about Byron, and had also told her off for leaving the party as she had. And Danielle had scolded her parent for not telling her about Rod. They had apparently met at a mutual friend's dinner party, much as she had thought.

Now it was Sunday, and she'd been for her usual morning ride. When she got home she was shocked to see Byron sitting on the paddock fence waiting for her.

'Good morning,' he called out cheerfully, as though it was perfectly normal for him to be there. 'What an early bird you are. I'd hoped to catch you before you went. I thought we could ride together.'

'Really?' Danielle tried not to show her pleasure.

Every inch of her had sprung into life. He looked fantastic in black jeans and polo shirt, and she couldn't understand why some other woman hadn't snapped him up. He was totally, totally male these days, irresistibly so; black really suited him, made him look mysterious and exciting and very, very sexy.

'Yes, really,' he answered.

'I thought you couldn't ride?'

'I was hoping you would teach me. There can't be much to it. Maybe after breakfast?' He looked at her optimistically.

'I don't think so.'

'You presume I couldn't learn?'

'It's not that—I'm sure you could—but—'

'You have other plans, then?' he asked fiercely, very fiercely, a deep frown dragging his thick brows together, his eyes narrowed on her face.

It wasn't difficult to guess what he was thinking. 'Actually, no, I'm doing nothing.' Though how she wished that she were.

'So why don't you want to spend time with me?'

'You know why,' Danielle thrust. Maybe she *should* have said that she was going out. It would be difficult now to get rid of him. Why couldn't he leave her alone? What was it going to take for him to get the message?

He followed her into the house and took it upon himself to cook breakfast while she showered and changed out of her jodhpurs. There was almost no point if they were going riding, but she needed space to get used to the idea that she would be spending the next several hours in Byron's company. Although she oughtn't to have let it, the thought filled her with pleasure. At the same time she knew the danger she was in.

She'd had a whole week to school herself, but the

moment she'd seen him sitting out there on the fence she'd known that she had failed miserably. Loving Byron came as naturally as breathing, and denying herself was going to be the hardest thing she had ever had to do.

They had their breakfast on the patio. Orange juice, scrambled eggs on toast and coffee. Food had never tasted so delicious.

After the storm last weekend the weather had turned hot again, and even now at a little after eight it was already quite warm. Or was it because of Byron? Danielle couldn't be sure.

'This is much better than my roof-top garden,' he said, drinking the last drops of his coffee and sitting back in his chair, replete. And almost to himself, 'I must give Sam a ring—make sure she isn't forgetting to water my plants.'

'She?' queried Danielle. It had never occurred to her that Sam was female. Not that it mattered; she obviously meant nothing to him or he wouldn't be chasing her, Danielle.

Byron smiled lazily. 'Didn't I tell you Sam's a girl?'

'No, you didn't, and you're very lucky to find someone to tend it for you.'

'I suppose I am. The fact is she really enjoys it.'

Danielle wondered if it was *only* Byron's garden Sam enjoyed looking after. 'Why don't you move out into the country if you like gardens so much?'

'Is that an invitation?' An eyebrow arched expectantly.

Danielle gave an inward groan; she had walked right into that. 'I don't mean here,' she said firmly.

'You have plenty of room,' he pointed out.

'I like being on my own.'

'Does your mysterious lover ever stay?'

She closed her eyes, as if by doing so she would not have to answer the question. Tony had never stayed. He'd wanted to, but she'd known that once she started that sort of a relationship she would feel compelled to marry him. Finally she looked at Byron and shook her head. 'No.'

'But I've no doubt that he'd like to?'

'Isn't that what all men want?' she retaliated.

Byron's nostrils flared in sudden anger and he looked as though he would like to pursue the conversation. Instead he jumped to his feet. 'Let's get ready to ride.'

'I think we should let our breakfast go down.'

He shrugged. 'OK, then, let's walk it off.'

'If you want to walk, then you go. I'll stay and wash up.'

'What's wrong with your dishwasher?' he growled.

'I don't use it now I'm on my own.'

'But you're not on your own, I'm here. And I shall be here for lunch and tea as well, so put them in the damn washer and let's get going.'

'You're staying the whole day?' Danielle's heart accelerated before it dropped into her shoes.

'You said you had no other plans.'

'But—'

'But nothing,' he said harshly.

They walked for a couple of miles, talking desultorily, Byron's black mood gradually dispersing. And when they got back she tacked up the two horses and invited Byron to mount Morgan.

'She's very gentle; you have nothing to worry about,' she told him.

He looked dubiously at the smaller horse. 'I'd prefer to ride Sandor.'

Danielle knew he was right, the mare was really too small for him, but Sandor was never happy about a stranger on his back, and he would sense that Byron had never ridden before.

'He might buck.'

'I'll risk it,' Byron said.

'You won't blame me if you get thrown?'

'No, I won't blame you.' And, so saying, he put his foot in the stirrup and mounted the bay easily.

Danielle had to admit he looked good on the horse, better than he would have done on Morgan. After she had given him a few quiet instructions, they moved off.

She had permission from a neighbouring farmer to ride on his land, and to her total amazement Sandor behaved himself beautifully. She found it difficult to believe that Byron had never ridden. He'd either been lying or he was a natural born rider; he seemed to know instinctively what to do.

He urged Sandor into a trot even before Danielle thought he was ready, and then broke into a canter. Danielle followed suit, calling to Byron to be careful. There was a row of bushes ahead, hidden for the moment in a dip. She knew that Sandor would jump them easily, but Byron would not be prepared, and if he fell off she had the feeling that he would lay all the blame on her.

Instead she was the one who fell. She had her eyes firmly fixed on Byron instead of looking where she was going. He and Sandor had taken the jump easily, but Morgan misjudged her stride and came to an abrupt halt when she realised that she was not going to make it. Danielle sailed over her head.

She managed to yell out before everything went black.

CHAPTER SEVEN

DANIELLE opened her eyes to find Byron leaning anxiously over her. She looked into his worried face and felt foolish. What a stupid thing to have done. But when she attempted to get up a firm hand pushed her back down. 'Stay where you are while I check for broken bones. Lord, you gave me one hell of a scare.'

'I'm all right,' she told him fiercely, not relishing the thought of his hands exploring her body. But when she scrambled to her feet the whole world spun, and if Byron had not steadied her she would have crashed back down.

He held her firmly against him. 'Maybe you haven't broken anything but you're certainly not well. You haven't an ounce of colour.'

'Was I out long?'

He shook his head. 'A minute, perhaps.'

'It's never happened to me before.' She was glad of the warmth and strength of his body. 'I've fallen, yes, but I've never knocked myself out.'

'I think we should get you straight home and call a doctor.'

'Rubbish,' declared Danielle firmly. 'I'll be fine.' Then she remembered the horses. 'Where's Morgan? Is she all right?'

Byron nodded and pointed, and Danielle saw both Sandor and Morgan standing nearby, watching her intently. She moved towards them and felt yet another wave of dizziness.

There was deep concern in Byron's voice. 'The sooner

you're home, the better, and as you're in no fit state to walk, we'll both ride Sandor.'

Danielle wanted to argue but knew he made sense. The journey seemed achingly long, Morgan trailing behind on a long rein, Sandor's saddle secured over her because it was easier for them to ride bareback, and for once Danielle was not even conscious of Byron.

On any other occasion she would have exhilarated in the feel of him against her, the smell of him, everything about him, but all she wanted at this moment was a long soak in the bath and then the bliss of her comfortable bed.

What she had not counted on was Byron helping her undress, Byron running her bath and helping her into it, Byron towelling her dry before slipping her nightie over her head and guiding her into bed.

She tried to tell herself that it did not matter, that he had seen everything hundreds of times before, and she tried to convince herself also that the feelings hurtling around her body were nothing to do with love and desire. She was too weary, ached too much to experience such sensations.

Sleep claimed her, and the next thing Danielle heard was Dr Jones's gentle voice. After giving her a thorough examination, he announced slight concussion and suggested she take it easy for a couple of days. 'You have someone to look after you? Your mother, perhaps?'

'There's no need to bother Danielle's mother,' declared Byron. 'I'll look after her.'

'Good.' Dr Jones saw nothing strange in that.

But when he had gone, Danielle sat up and glared. 'How dare you?'

'How dare I what?' asked Byron innocently.

'I don't want you here. I can look after myself, thank you very much.'

'You heard what the good doctor said. Rest, and plenty of it. I think you should stay in bed for the rest of the day.'

'I can do that without you,' she retorted.

'What about the horses? Who'll look after them? You need me, Danielle, whether you like it or not. Of course, if you'd prefer your mother... Though, somehow I don't think she'll be very happy to discover I've been out riding with you. She'll probably blame me for your fall.'

Which she would, Danielle knew, and the thought of her mother waltzing around her bed, going into a whole diatribe about Byron, was more than she could stomach. She slid back beneath the covers and closed her eyes. 'You win,' she muttered unhappily.

Danielle slept for most of the day, or at least she pretended to. Byron constantly popped in and out, but always she kept her eyes resolutely closed. Sometimes he sat down on the chair next to her bed and it was hell trying to feign sleep. Sometimes he brushed her hair back from her forehead with warm, gentle fingers and need flared within her.

For her lunch he made soup, and for her supper steamed fish. 'Anyone would think I was an invalid,' she grumbled, and yet deep down inside she enjoyed the attention he was lavishing on her.

He would not let her get up, except to go to the bathroom, and when she suggested it was time he returned to his hotel he told her that he was staying the night.

'You can't!' she exclaimed in horror.

'Why not?'

'Because, because...' she foundered.

'Because you're afraid?' he taunted softly.

'Because I don't need you. I'm all right now.'

'Maybe.' An eyebrow quirked as he studied her. 'But I'm staying. After all the whole thing is my fault. If I hadn't asked to ride none of this would have happened.'

Danielle clamped her lips and her heartbeat grew unsteady, and she knew she would get no sleep that night. She would be too busy wondering whether Byron was sleeping, whether he would find his way into her room—and ultimately her bed! It did not bear thinking about.

In the end she was worrying for nothing. Byron brought her up a mug of drinking chocolate at ten o'clock, made sure there was nothing else she wanted, gave her a brief kiss on the cheek, and she did not see him again until the following morning.

She heard him, though. It was about midnight before he came to bed. He used the bathroom opposite and then let himself into the bedroom next to hers. He tried to be quiet, but she heard the tiny sounds of him moving about and undressing, and the grunt he gave when he dropped into bed. They were familiar sounds and it drove home the fact of how much she missed him, how much she wanted him, how much he meant to her.

That night she dreamt of Byron, she dreamt of what might have been—of children and laughter, of love and happiness, all that was denied her now—and when she woke in the cold light of dawn tears streamed unchecked down her cheeks.

She heard Byron get up and go downstairs, and immediately she went into the bathroom and washed her face. The last thing she wanted was him asking questions. By the time he came to see if she was awake, she had brushed her hair and was sitting up in bed with a welcoming smile pasted to her lips.

'A vast improvement, I would say,' were his first words.

Danielle inclined her head. 'I feel much better. Back to normal in fact.'

'If you're suggesting I leave you to your own devices you can forget it,' he said firmly. 'I know what will happen the moment my back's turned. I'll go and get your breakfast.'

Danielle wanted to say that she would get up for it but he had already gone, and a few minutes later a laden tray was set down in front of her. Freshly squeezed orange juice, lightly browned toast and a coddled egg, her best china teapot, and a single red rose!

It was the rose that bothered her. It said so much. And, it coming on top of her dream, she felt the sting of tears again. 'You've gone to a lot of trouble,' she said huskily. 'Thank you.'

'Just make sure you eat it all. Shall I pour your tea?'

Was there a gruffness to his voice too? Had he observed her reaction? Did he know how she felt? 'I can manage,' she said softly.

'In that case I'll go and eat my own breakfast.' He hesitated, as though hoping she might suggest he join her, but when she remained silent he turned and left.

She stared for long moments at the rose. He was telling her yet again that he loved her, and she wished he wouldn't; she wished he would go away and leave her alone. She had told him enough times that there was no place for him in her life; she had hinted that there was someone else. What more would it take?

Danielle nibbled her toast and sipped her tea but her heart wasn't in it, and when Byron returned the tray was pushed to one side.

He frowned. 'Something wrong with the food?'

'No.'

'You're not hungry?'

'No.'

'Why not?'

'Because lying in bed hardly works up an appetite,' she retorted irritably. 'I'm getting up.'

If she had expected opposition, she got none. 'Very well, but you're still to be careful.'

'I know—no riding, nothing energetic. I'll just laze around the house, maybe dead-head a few roses.' Roses! Why had she brought them into the conversation?

'And you can watch me mow your lawns.'

Danielle groaned inwardly; she didn't want him doing anything for her. 'I'm grateful for the time you've spent with me, Byron, but you have your own work to consider. I'll be all right now.'

'Such politeness! What you're really saying is that you don't like me in your house. Maybe it's loverboy you'd rather have looking after you, mmm? The mystery man who never seems to be around. Would you like me to phone him?'

'You're being ridiculous, Byron.'

'Am I?' he countered fiercely. 'Will he be happy when he knows I've stayed the night? Or won't you tell him? Will that be our little secret? Does he know that your ex is on the scene again? How much *does* he know, Ellie? Anything? Or nothing at all?' And when she didn't answer, 'You haven't told him, have you? Why? Afraid he'll be jealous? Afraid it will cause problems between you? Do you think—?'

'Shut up!' Danielle could stand his taunts no longer. 'If you must know, he's working abroad.'

'And I'm expected to believe that?' he asked contemptuously. 'The same as I was supposed to believe that your husband was away? Do you know what I think, Ellie? I think that he exists only in your imagination— as a defence against me.'

Danielle closed her eyes for a brief second. 'You can believe what you like, Byron, but Tony does exist, I assure you. Now, if you wouldn't mind, I'd like to get dressed.'

'Tony?'

'That's right.'

'Tony who?'

'Does it matter?'

'I want to know.'

Danielle shrugged. 'Tony Cochran. Does that make a difference? Is he real now? Do you want to know anything else about him? Date of birth? Address? National Insurance number? What he—?'

'OK.' He held up his hand. 'You've made your point.'

'So you believe me?'

He nodded, and Danielle saw defeat behind his eyes as he picked up her tray and left the room.

She collapsed back against the pillows. Now that she had finally convinced him there was no hope, she felt unutterably sad. It was for the best, the only solution, and yet the thought of never seeing him again was the worst torture imaginable. He had become a part of her life again; the void would be enormous when he was no longer there.

It was several minutes before she summoned the energy to drag herself out of bed, and even longer still before she made her way downstairs. The rest of the day was sheer hell.

Byron was friendly enough; he was attentive to her every need, in fact, but with a detachment that was not normally there, and with a blankness in his eyes that she found distressing. He treated her as a friend, not a potential lover, not as the woman he loved.

He no longer flirted or charmed her with provocative gestures or words, and after a delicious dinner of pork fillet with a wonderful sauce he had whipped up—to which neither of them did justice—he announced his intention of returning to the hotel. 'I think you're well enough to be left now.'

Danielle nodded. 'You've been very kind.' Banal words, not what she really meant, not enough to convey her real feelings.

'I'd have done the same for anyone.'

Bathed anyone? Undressed anyone? The thought cut deep. She hoped he was only saying it to hide his own disappointment, his own hurt.

His goodnight kiss was perfunctory, and after he had gone the house felt dreadfully empty. She kept expecting to see him, to hear him pottering around in the kitchen, or for him to call out to her, and when she went to bed she kept imagining him in the room next to hers. It was awful, and she was glad he hadn't slept in her bed because that would have made it even worse.

In the emptiness of the days that followed she felt as low as when she had walked out on their marriage. It had taken a lot of guts at the time but it had been the right thing to do. She had done it for Byron's sake, and it was right now that he had walked out on her. There was no future for them together. She must bundle her love back into the deepest recesses of her mind, lock the door, and get on with her life.

It was not easy, and whenever the doorbell rang over the next few days her heart quickened its beat, just in case it was him. It never was.

She spent extra time at the shop, even talked to

Melissa about opening another one, she took her horses out more often, but the pain did not go away.

And then one evening just over a week later her doorbell rang, and when she saw the shape of a man through the patterned glass—a tall, broad shouldered man—she flew to it with a smile on her lips and her heart thumping fit to burst.

Her smile quickly faded when she realised it wasn't Byron.

'Aren't you pleased to see me?'

'Tony! I'm sorry, of course I am. It's just that I was expecting someone else.' She replaced her smile and held out her hand in welcome. 'Come in. This is a surprise. Are they quick learners in Malaysia? Have you finished there already?'

He dropped his suitcase just inside the door. 'How about giving me a kiss and I'll answer your questions later?'

He was taller than Byron and much more heavily built, and yet there was a surprising gentleness about him. He had a round face and soft brown eyes, and when he held her it was like being enclosed in something safe and warm and comfortable. Which was all right if that was what you wanted, but they weren't the sort of feelings that Byron aroused in her, that made her feel special, ultra-feminine, sensual, as though she was walking ten feet off the ground.

Tony's kiss, though pleasant, did nothing for her, and Danielle knew that she had been right to constantly turn down his proposals of marriage. And if he had come for his final answer he was going to be one very disappointed man.

'A cup of tea?' she asked, pulling gently away. 'Or a beer?' She missed the shadow that crossed his face.

'A beer, I think, and a favour. I need somewhere to sleep. It's been a heck of a long day, the flight alone was extremely long, and I'm dog-tired. I hate hotels, and I've rented my place out, so—'

'Tony, of course you can have a bed here.' She had always fought shy of letting him stay before in case he asked too much of her, but this was different.

She poured his beer and a gin and tonic for herself, and they sat in the lounge. 'Did you enjoy Malaysia?' she asked.

'Did I enjoy it?' Tony's smile said everything. 'It's a wonderful, beautiful country, and the people are so friendly, especially towards the English. I'm staying in a condominium that has two storeys and a spiral staircase and views over the sea. It's absolute luxury.'

'Will you mind staying longer?'

'I think that's up to you, Danielle.'

Was that the reason he was back now? Because he wanted an answer from her? His infrequent letters over the last three months—by his own admission he wasn't much of a letter writer—had made no mention of marriage, for which she'd been thankful, but he had always signed his letters 'with love for ever'.

'But we won't talk about that now,' he added. 'There's plenty of time.'

Plenty of time! What did that mean? 'How long are you going to be in England?' she asked with a faint frown.

'A week maximum, I would think,' he answered. 'I've been recalled to do a special job. It shouldn't take long.'

And he wanted to stay with her for the whole time? She wasn't sure she would have said yes had she known.

He had a sandwich and another beer, and finally he yawned and announced that he was ready for bed.

Danielle was tired too and so they went upstairs together. He'd once done some decorating for her so he knew exactly which room was hers, and he hesitated when they reached it, a questioning lift to his brows.

Danielle shook her head and gave him a brief peck on the cheek. 'Your room's next door, Tony. Goodnight.' And she slid quickly inside.

This time, as she lay in bed, she did not listen for any tell-tale movements. She wondered instead how she could tell Tony that she could never marry him without hurting his feelings too much. And now it wasn't only because she didn't want to saddle him with a wife who could bear him no children, it was because of Byron. She had never stopped loving him; she never would. There could be no other man in her life. She had to resign herself to that fact.

The next morning Tony still looked heavy-eyed, as though he could do with a few more hours' sleep before going to work. 'I don't know what time I'll be back,' he said as he shrugged into his jacket after breakfast, adding concernedly, 'It is all right, me staying with you?'

Danielle nodded, even though she would have liked to say no, and he was on his way out before it occurred to her that she ought to give him a key. She ran after him. 'You'd better take this.'

She wasn't prepared when he wrapped her in one of his bear-like hugs, his lips finding hers. 'I've missed you, Danielle. I—'

They both turned as they heard a car door slam—loudly.

'It looks as though you have a visitor,' he said. 'I'd better be off. See you later, sweetheart.'

Danielle watched in disbelief as Byron walked towards her, passing Tony, not so much as looking at the other man but fixing Danielle with hostile eyes instead.

'So loverboy's back!' He strode into the house, and when the door was closed he swung to face her, his eyes condemning. 'You both look as though you've had one hell of a night. I'd suggest you mix a little sleep with it in future.'

Infuriated that he had charged in without waiting to be asked, her voice was equally cutting. 'You don't know what you're talking about.' The fact that *she* looked washed out had certainly nothing to do with Tony, and a whole lot to do with Byron. 'I thought I'd got rid of you,' she thrust furiously. 'Why are you back?'

'I was just asking myself the same question.' His nostrils flared as he spoke, eyes narrowing until they were no more than calculating silver slits.

'You must have a reason for being here?'

'Judging by what I've just seen,' he sneered, 'my reason is of no importance.'

'Then maybe you should turn around and leave,' she suggested coolly. Lord, this was crucifying. Her nerves were twanging, her blood racing. The mere sight of him aroused every base instinct. Nothing had ever prepared her for the pain of loving a man who could never be hers.

Had he come with the sole intention of trying again? Had he thought that with time to think things over she would decide that she could not live without him?

She closed her eyes briefly, and was taken by surprise when his hands clamped her shoulders. 'How long has this been going on?' he wanted to know.

'How long has what been going on? You already know about Tony.'

'You didn't tell me that you slept with him,' he

snorted, eyes hard and impaling, making it impossible for her to look away.

'Is that what you think?' She swallowed hard and held his gaze.

'It's what it looks like. Are you going to deny it?'

Danielle shook her head. 'You wouldn't believe me if I did.'

'Too true, I wouldn't,' he growled, and still his fingers punished.

His nearness was almost her undoing. She wanted to press her body against his, to feel the exciting warmth and hardness, to be kissed by him, to share racing hearts and quickening pulses. To become one. But it was forbidden. It was like the apple in the Garden of Eden. One bite and it would change her world for ever.

Please go away. Her brain transmitted the impulse. Please leave me alone. Please don't torture me any more.

Byron heard nothing, and Danielle doubted he would have heeded if he had.

Suddenly, without warning, one hand cradled the back of her head, the other the small of her back, and almost before she knew what was happening, certainly before she could stop him, his mouth captured hers.

It was what she wanted and yet it wasn't. Flames soared and yet she knew she must resist. She could not allow this; it was dangerous, it was insane, it had no place in her life. She spread her hands on his chest and pushed with all her might.

She felt the strong beat of his heart, she felt muscle and heat and pulsing desire. Desire! She pushed harder. She had to put space between them before physical feelings took over.

It was hard to withstand when his lips moved ever more urgently over hers, when his tongue forced its way into her mouth, reacquainting itself with the moist recesses it had once known so well.

'Tell me,' he muttered thickly, angrily, 'how I compare with loverboy. Does he excite you like I do?'

The beat of her heart was like hammer blows within her chest; blood roared in her ears, pulses pounded. Get away from me! Get away from me! The words rang in her head but once again failed to find their way to the surface.

Her efforts to free herself were in vain; his arms tightened and his mouth continued to demand, lifting only briefly to growl, 'You haven't answered my question, Danielle.'

Danielle, not Ellie! Proving he was angry with her. She put every ounce of energy into holding out against him. It was harder than anything she'd ever had to do. But from somewhere she found the strength, and when, in a sudden blaze of anger, Byron pushed her roughly from him she felt bereft instead of triumphant, and almost lost her footing as she stumbled backwards across the room.

'Had too much of a good thing last night, did you?' he jeered.

She could see the rage in his eyes, the frustration. Her lack of response was a first, and he felt humiliated.

'Trying to tell me that I'm not good enough for you? Well, have I got news for you, sweet ex-wife of mine! You didn't fool me for one minute. You were dying to respond; Lord knows what sort of a twisted mind controlled you.' His lips curled contemputously. 'And, having seen loverboy, I refuse to believe that you think more of him than you do me. He's not your type. And nor was John, if it comes to that.'

Danielle lifted her head and eyed him with equal contempt. 'Are you suggesting that you have the monopoly on my emotions? Be realistic, Byron Meredith. I rid my mind of you many years ago.'

A dark brow quirked. 'I'm expected to believe that, after the few demonstrations I've had recently?'

'Physical responses don't count,' she pointed out. 'I don't deny you're an attractive man. But that's not the issue. I'll spell it out to you for one last time: Go! Keep away from me! I don't want you to be a part of my life.' She spoke quietly, calmly, amazing even herself because inside she was churning like an ocean in a force-ten gale.

'That might not be so easy.'

Danielle looked at him suspiciously.

'JBS is in trouble. Big trouble. They're being held responsible for the problems with the gallery.'

'But the builders—Scotts—aren't they—?'

'Have gone out of business,' he cut in tersely. 'An extraordinary board meeting has been called for ten-thirty. It's why I'm here. If you will please get ready we'll leave.'

'But you're not on the board,' she protested. And why hadn't Rod told her himself?

'Rod thought that under the circumstances I should be present. I have my good name to defend.'

'And he left it to you to tell me?' she asked derisively.

'Only because I offered.' He made it sound like plain, simple common sense, and yet Danielle knew there was more to it than that. He had used it as an excuse, an excuse to see her again. What he hadn't bargained on was finding her with another man.

CHAPTER EIGHT

BYRON had not wanted to believe Danielle's story that there was someone else in her life. Because she spent so much time alone, he had decided that there couldn't possibly be anyone, that he was an invention designed to keep him at bay. Even when she'd said he was working abroad and had given him a name, he had found it difficult to accept.

Coming face to face with him, though, especially first thing in the morning when it was obvious that he had spent the night in her bed—something she had not allowed him to do—had been like a sharp slap on the face. Worse than that, even—like being dunked in a whole bathful of icy cold water.

He had seen the kiss they'd given each other, the softly spoken words, the easy familiarity. The tableau would remain with him for ever. He had no hope now of a reconciliation. There seemed little point in even trying, and yet he knew that he had to, that he could not give up. Not unless she actually married again and was thus forbidden to him. If that happened then—

'What do you think, Byron?'

'I'm sorry?' He gave himself a mental shake and came back to the present.

The meeting continued.

Danielle made very little contribution, avoiding looking at him even when he addressed the whole room. Her lack of response when he had kissed her earlier, and her total silence in the car, had both served to tell him that he was wasting his time, that she was determined to shut him out of her life. He was equally determined not to allow it—even more so now that he had seen Tony Cochran. How could she love a big hulk of a man like that?

It was half past twelve before the board meeting came to a close, and Byron had no intention of taking Danielle straight home. When he headed into the city centre itself instead of out towards Henley he expected opposition. She did not disappoint him.

'Where are we going?' Her tone was sharp, her eyes flashing their incredible blue.

'It's lunchtime,' he announced pleasantly. Her perfume drugged and tantalised him as always and she looked ravishing in an ice-blue suit with a darker camisole beneath. Her hair, sleek and shiny and the colour of a fox, was tempting to touch. He would have liked to take her to bed rather than for a meal, but he knew that this was off the agenda for a long time yet. He refused to think it might never happen. Never was too long.

'But I've made plans,' she protested.

'Then you're going to have to break them,' he told her decisively. 'If it's loverboy you can ring him. Tell him some business has cropped up.' He found it difficult to hide his disapproval.

Danielle's face tightened and her fingers curled into fists. 'Don't you ever take no for an answer?'

'Not where you're concerned,' he told her calmly.

'I thought you had.'

'Then you thought wrong.'

'You think you know what's best for me, is that it? You don't approve of Tony?' Her voice was high and accusing. 'Well, let me tell you, Byron Mere—'

'Danielle.' He reached out and placed his hand over

hers. 'There's no need to get steamed up. It's just lunch. I'm not about to make any heavy demands.'

'Yet,' she proclaimed, and he knew she was thinking about the way he had kissed her this morning. It had been a mistake—a big one. But he had needed to confirm that her feelings for him had not died. Her lack of response had sent slivers of fear crawling down his spine.

He slid the car neatly into a metred parking space as another car left, well aware that Danielle probably knew this area a whole lot better than he did. He was aware also that she might have eaten with Tony at the same waterside pub he had in mind.

He took her hand and led her down to Brindley Place, to part of Birmingham's thirty-three-mile canal system which had undergone a dramatic change since his student days. It had been in danger of falling into decay, but was now a thriving, award-winning area filled with cafés and restaurants as well as a few shops. He'd hardly been able to believe his eyes when he'd first seen the transformation.

'You've been here before?' he asked.

Danielle nodded. 'But not to eat, and I'm not hungry now.' She tried to tug her hand out of his.

He was not letting her go. 'I'm sure you'll change your mind.'

The whole area was overlooked by the imposing International Convention Centre with its magnificent Symphony Hall, and the equally impressive tall hotel in which he was staying, with its hundreds of mirrored windows.

'I wish I'd been asked to help design this place,' he said. 'The developers have done a magnificent job, don't you think? It's totally transformed.' There were views from parts of the canal that made Birmingham's skyline look like a mini-Manhattan.

'It is quite remarkable,' she agreed. 'I've watched it grow.'

They decided to eat at the Malthouse. They sat upstairs on a long open balcony where they could look down at the colourful narrowboats passing leisurely by, and at the Sea Life Centre opposite, where visitors walked through a transparent tunnel and saw sharks and rays swimming all around them.

'What would you like to drink?' Byron asked.

'Tonic water,' she replied flatly.

He was almost afraid to leave her while he went to the bar—in case she got up and left—but when he looked back she was studying the menu. When he placed her drink in front of her she did not even glance at him, just said a quiet thank you.

It pained him to see shadows beneath her eyes that had not been there before. She looked thinner and paler too, and he went cold at the thought that her pallor was caused by nights of passion instead of healthy, rejuvenating sleep. He wished that he had taken the opportunity to punch the big guy on the jaw instead of walking straight past him. It was what he had wanted to do, only sanity and good sense had prevented him.

She finally decided on the seafood basket, and he on the steak and scampi combo, but she still refused to meet his eyes, and he had to reach out and touch her to make her look at him. 'Is something troubling you, Danielle?'

She shook her head.

'Thinking about loverboy?' The words were out before he could stop them, sneering words which made him feel uncomfortable. What was the matter with him? He oughtn't to treat her like this, not if he wanted her on his side.

'His name is Tony,' she hissed through her teeth.

'OK,' he shrugged, 'Tony it is. Tell me about him.' He wanted to know everything. How long they had known each other, what they meant to each other, what his intentions were. *What they did together!*

'Why should I?' she retorted.

'Because I'm interested.'

'I bet you are,' she snapped. 'As interested as you'd be in a basket of wet fish.'

Ouch! But he deserved it, he supposed. He had been less than complimentary about her friend. 'Is it serious between you?'

Danielle's incredible blue eyes, intensified by the blue of her camisole, flashed hostilely. 'If I said yes would you leave me alone?'

'I think you know the answer to that,' he answered quietly. And those entrancing freckles. He wanted to kiss each and every one of them.

A further fiery blue flash. 'Then I see no reason why I should tell you. My relationship with Tony concerns no one but me. If the only reason you've brought me here is to pump me about him, then you can forget it.' She pushed back her wrought-iron chair and stood up.

'Ellie.' Byron mentally kicked himself. He must really exercise caution. 'Please sit down. I shouldn't have questioned you; I'm sorry.'

'Are you?' she snapped.

'Yes, I am.' He held her eyes for a few moments, and was relieved when she slowly and reluctantly dropped back into her chair. 'But I do think you ought to phone him if you've made plans to—'

'I wasn't seeing him; I was doing something else. It's not vitally important; it will wait.'

He was pleased that she hadn't been going to meet Tony, and for a few minutes they sat in silence. Danielle watched the boats, and he looked at a new development of luxurious town houses and apartments just a little way further along the canal. He'd been told there were penthouses there, and he amused himself wondering how Danielle would feel if he said that he was going to come and live in one of them.

After their meal arrived he tried to make further amends. 'I wasn't prying, Ellie, at least that was not my intention. It was friendly curiosity, that's all.'

She threw him a look of scorn, clearly not believing a word.

'Let's forget your friend, shall we?' he suggested hurriedly. 'Tell me what you've been doing since I last saw you.'

'Do you mean have I been seeing a lot of Tony?' she asked coldly, stabbing a prawn as though it were still alive and she was trying to kill it.

Oh, Lord, he couldn't say the right thing. 'I don't mean that at all. I mean have you been riding? How's Morgan? No ill effects after the fall? And yourself—no repercussions? You look a little pale. You didn't do too much too soon?'

'No, I didn't, and I'm well.' Her tones were clipped. 'How about you, Byron?'

She was saying nothing and he didn't blame her. He shouldn't have jumped in so quickly and started asking questions. The trouble was he wanted to know every tiny thing she had done. He wanted to know how she had coped when he'd left her, whether she'd thought about him, whether she missed him, whether she dreamt about him, longed for him in her bed at night.

Or did Tony Cochran surpass him? Was he a better lover? Better at everything? Did she love Tony more than she had ever loved him? Had she loved John more? She had once hinted that this was the case. It didn't bear thinking about. His blood began to boil and he knew he had to be careful.

He took a couple of deep, steadying breaths. 'As a matter of fact I've been in London.' He had returned to Birmingham when the private detective he'd hired said he had some important news for him, but it was not something he could discuss with Danielle yet, not until he had the whole picture. Even then he would have to be careful, because if it was true he did not know how she would take it.

'I see. Rod phoned and told you about the meeting?'

Byron nodded. It was best to let her think this was his reason for coming back.

'Have you any more exciting projects in the pipeline?'

He didn't blame her for steering the conversation away from all things personal. 'As a matter of fact I've just been offered the opportunity to design a brand-new shopping centre in Paris,' he told her. 'Something exclusive and stylish for the very rich. It should be quite a challenge.'

'Paris?' Her eyes opened incredibly wide.

He nodded. 'I'm flying over there tomorrow to look at the site.' He wished he could invite her to go with him.

'Have you finished here now that it's finally agreed it's not a design fault?'

In truth he had, but because of Tony he couldn't afford to take a back seat. He had done that when he'd gone to university; he was not about to make the same mistake again. 'I guess I'll still be paying fairly frequent visits until the remedial work's done. After all, it is one of my babies.'

He saw the sudden tightening of her lips, the unhappiness in her eyes which she was quick to mask. She couldn't have made it any plainer that she did not welcome his presence. Would he make an even bigger fool of himself if he sought her out again? Ought he to let go? Accept the inevitable? But he knew he could not do that. He could not give up without a fight.

The meal was over, and Danielle breathed a sigh of relief. Hiding her feelings was one of the hardest things she had ever had to do, but she was confident that she had succeeded, that Byron had no inkling that she was still in love with him. In fact she was doing such a good job of it that she had almost convinced herself.

And thankfully Byron had stopped talking about Tony. It was wrong of her to pretend that he meant more to her than he did, but what else could she do? It seemed to be working, and that was all that mattered.

On the way home Danielle was so deep in thought that it didn't strike her straight away that he had driven straight through Henley-in-Arden. Crossly she swung round in her seat. 'You've missed my turning.'

He smiled. 'I thought we'd go into Stratford as it's such a nice afternoon, maybe take a boat out on the river.'

'Without even asking whether I want to go?'

'I knew what your answer would be,' he confessed. 'So I thought I'd make the decision for you.'

It was both heaven and hell. Of course she wanted to spend time with him; she wanted to spend the rest of her life with him. But it was something she must out of necessity deny herself.

At this precise moment she had no choice, but after today she would make it *absolutely* clear that she did not want to see him again—*ever*. If Tony wasn't enough of a deterrent, then she would find some other solution.

Their conversation was about anything and everything except their own feelings. He told her how proud he had been when he'd become a fully fledged architect, about the invaluable help and advice he had received from his mentor, Joseph O'Flannery, and about some of his successes since.

He described his London penthouse, which sounded fabulous, and she felt sad that she would never see it. 'Sam's done marvels with the plants,' he added. 'They've never looked so good. I think I ought to give her the permanent job.'

In return she told him about opening her shop in Birmingham and worrying herself to death because she feared that it would be a flop. 'I thought I had started too big. That maybe I should have opened in Henley and then gone on to Birmingham later.'

'And you worried for nothing?'

She nodded. 'I'm actually now thinking of opening another.' Now, why had she said that? It was something she wanted to do to take her mind off Byron, not include him in it.

'You are?' The interest in his face confirmed her mistake. 'Where?'

'I haven't made up my mind; I need to look around.'

'Still in Birmingham?'

'I don't think so. Maybe in Redditch or Stratford, even.' They were both only eight miles away. Much nearer than Birmingham in fact.

'William Shakespeare's birthplace is an excellent choice,' he said. 'It's always busy. You should do well there. We could look to see if there are any suitable premises while we're there,' he added enthusiastically.

'I don't think so,' replied Danielle. Byron's help was the last thing she wanted.

'It's going to take up a lot of your time.'

'I don't mind that.'

'It won't be too much for you?'

'No.'

He went quiet, and she knew he was thinking about Tony, probably dying to ask whether she intended enlisting his help.

It didn't take them long to reach Stratford, but it took them ages to find a parking spot. It was thronged with people and they had to queue to take a rowing boat out on the river. But it was fun; Danielle could not deny that she was enjoying herself, especially when she had a go at rowing.

Afterwards they wandered along the banks of the Avon, watching other boaters, watching children play on the short-cropped grass. When a ball came bouncing towards them, Byron kicked it back and spent a few moments joining in the boys' football game. And when a tiny tot started to cry because she was lost, Byron was the first to pick her up and scour the area until he found her mother—who had not even realised that she was missing!

It was plain to see how much he adored children, how good he was with them—how they in their turn adored him. He was a natural with them, and it was criminal to think of landing him with a lifestyle where he could never have any of his own. If today's outing had done nothing else it had reinforced what she already knew.

They had tea and scones with clotted cream and strawberry jam in a little café, and it was very pleasant, but all Danielle wanted to do was go home and shut her door and put an end to this torture.

When they'd first met he had been equally ruthless in his pursuit of her—not that she had put up any resistance—but it was different now. She was being forced to fight him because of circumstances beyond her control. And it was destroying her. The only way she would get any peace was by driving him away permanently.

'You're very deep in thought.' They'd left the tea-shop, and Byron's stride was adjusted to hers as they strolled through the streets that were slightly less busy.

He made no attempt to touch her or even hold her hand, but he didn't have to; his nearness was disturbing enough. Invisible waves radiated from him to her, giving off signals that she did not want to pick up.

'What are you thinking about?'

'This and that,' she said.

'Would it include me?'

Danielle nodded.

'And, judging by your expression, they're not happy thoughts?'

'It's not my choice that I'm here.'

He slowed his steps and turned her to face him. 'The world was once our oyster. What happened, Ellie? What happened to us?' He sounded as desolate as she felt.

She looked reluctantly into his thickly lashed eyes. 'We didn't take the time to get to know each other. We jumped into marriage with both feet. It was a mistake.' And the best answer she could come up with.

He shook his head sadly. 'One day you were there, the next gone. Your clothes, everything. There was nothing left to remind me of you. Have you any idea how I felt?'

Danielle's heartbeat quickened. 'I left you a note.'

'Which explained nothing,' he derided shortly. '"It isn't working," you said. "I'm getting out." Can you imagine what that did to me? I went through hell.'

Nothing compared to the hell she had gone through.

'And I still don't know what I did to turn you against me.'

'It was nothing you did,' she said quietly.

'Then why, for pity's sake?'

Danielle shook her head and carried on walking.

Byron overtook and forced her to face him again. 'I'm not giving up without an answer, Ellie.'

She took a deep breath and, hating the lie, said, 'The truth is I fell out of love with you—if I ever was.'

'What do you mean "if"?' he ground out savagely.

'I think I might have mistaken infatuation for love. You swept me off my feet; you didn't give me time to think.' She kept her eyes resolutely on his chest as she spoke, conscious of groups of shoppers watching them curiously.

'Rubbish!' he snarled. 'I don't believe you.'

'So why would I walk out on you if I loved you?' she parried.

'You tell me,' he said. 'It's the mystery of the decade. For almost ten years I've puzzled over it. I've gone over every conversation we've ever had, everything we've ever done, and found no valid reason. But there has to be one, and I refuse to believe that you never loved me in the first place.'

Danielle grimaced. 'You don't agree that people can mistake lust for love?'

'Lust?' he asked disbelievingly. 'You're saying that's what it was?'

She nodded. 'Physical desire.' And God forgive her for lying.

'But it was love you felt for John?'

She swallowed hard and said quietly, 'Yes.' Because she *had* loved him after a fashion. Nothing like the love she'd felt for Byron, of course, but a quiet, safe love all the same.

'And Tony? You love him too?' He'd gone absolutely still by now, the whole world around them forgotten. They were in their own tiny universe.

Tears began to sting the backs of her eyes, but Danielle refused to let them fall. She nodded again, unable to put this second lie into words.

'Dammit.' Byron was almost dancing on the spot in his anger. 'You can't do this to me; I won't let you.'

'It's time you let go, Byron,' she said, her voice almost a whisper.

'I won't; I refuse to. You're mine, Danielle. All mine. You love me, I know you do, and, by hell, I'm going to prove it.'

Danielle thought for one moment that he was going to pull her into his arms right in front of their audience and kiss her and kiss her until she agreed that she loved him. But he didn't. Instead he took her hand and began to drag her along the pavement. She was forced to run to keep up with him, and when they reached the car he pushed her into it, and then drove as though all the hounds in hell were after him.

She presumed he was taking her home, presumed that this was where their conversation would continue. She wanted to tell him to ease up—she feared for their safety—but in the end she didn't have to. He slowed his pace of his own accord, but his face was still grim, his hands tense on the wheel.

Rush-hour traffic slowed their progress several times, and his fingers tapped the steering wheel impatiently whenever he was forced to stop. Neither said a word; Danielle because she knew ordinary, everyday conversation was out of the question, and Byron because he was too busy concentrating on the road—or because he wanted to wait until they were in the house.

No doubt he was going over and over in his mind exactly what he was going to say to her and how he was going to convince her that she was in love with him. She hoped that he was not going to use his body to persuade her because that would be her undoing. Having spent the entire day with him, having suffered a depth of emotions too enormous to contemplate, she would be unable to put up any further resistance.

He pulled up on her drive, killed the engine and then jumped out and waited impatiently while she fumbled for her house key. When she found it he took it from her and swung open the door. They stepped inside and he shut it again. 'Now, Danielle…' he began.

A faint cough at the top of the stairs made them both look up. Tony, wearing only a towel around his hips, his body still wet from the shower, looked down at them.

CHAPTER NINE

DANIELLE saw Byron's look of disbelief, heard his hiss of angry resignation, before he spun on his heel and wrenched open the door. In seconds he had gone.

She remained rooted to the spot.

Tony spoke. 'I'm sorry. I heard your key in the lock and thought I'd better let you know I was here. I expected you to be alone. Your friend looked a bit shocked. Ought you to go after him?'

'I don't think so. Why is your car not outside?' She frowned, trying to work out why Tony should be here when his car wasn't.

'It's in for repairs,' he told her. 'The clutch went this morning.' And then, looking down at his towel, 'I think I'd better make myself decent.'

Danielle had actually forgotten in the mad ride home that Tony might be here. But in fact he had done her a favour. Byron was convinced now that she and Tony were lovers.

She headed for the kitchen, but her actions were slow as she filled the kettle. Byron had gone. She would never see him again. It was what she wanted, what she'd planned, what was best, and yet she felt desolate. She sat down at the breakfast bar, laid her head on her hands, and let the tears flow.

Tony's concerned voice penetrated her misery a few minutes later.

'Danielle,' he said, 'whatever's the matter? Why are you crying? Who was that man? Has he something to do with it?' He took the stool next to her and put his arm across her shoulders.

She lifted her head and looked at him sadly, mopping her eyes on a sheet of kitchen roll. 'It was Byron.' She didn't have to explain; Tony knew everything, including her innermost thoughts—except how much she loved him! She hadn't known that herself until recently.

'I had no idea he'd turned up again. Is he a—permanent part of your life?'

Danielle saw the pain behind his eyes which he did his best to hide.

'No, he isn't,' she informed him gently. 'He'd like to be, but he isn't.'

'Have you told him about the baby yet? About the fact that you—?'

'No,' she cut in fiercely. 'And I'm never going to.'

Tony lifted his straggly brows reprovingly. 'But if seeing him is upsetting you this much then I think you should—'

'If I told Byron it would upset him too,' she retorted defensively. 'I'm doing it for his sake, not mine.' She slid down off the stool. 'A cup of tea?'

He nodded and said nothing more until she placed their drinks on the counter and rejoined him.

'I think Byron should be the one to decide whether—'

'Tony!' she exclaimed. 'It's my life; I shall do with it as I wish.'

'Are you still in love with him?' He asked the question sadly, as though he already knew what her answer was going to be.

She nodded and put her hand on his arm. 'I'm sorry.'

'Is that why you keep turning me down? Because deep inside your heart you know that—?'

'Heavens, no,' she jumped in quickly. 'I always

thought my feelings for Byron had died a natural death.' This wasn't strictly true, but it seemed the kindest thing to say. Tony was such a wonderful man that she hated hurting him. 'It's because you deserve a wife who can give you children. I can't marry any man, not ever again; you know that.'

'I think you're wrong, but...' He shrugged and let it rest. 'How long has Byron been around?'

'A few weeks,' she told him. 'We met accidentally and now he keeps turning up. Nothing's ever arranged. I didn't expect him today.'

'Do you think he'll be back?'

Danielle shook her head. 'I don't think so. I had actually told him about you, Tony. I'm afraid I let him think that we...' She grimaced as she tailed off. Honesty was the best policy, so it was said, but it was making her feel like a louse. 'I'm sorry if I'm hurting you. The thing is, you did me a big favour when you appeared half-naked on the stairs.'

'You should have gone after him, Danielle. You should have told him the truth. Just because you can't have kids it's no reason to—'

'Tony.' She laid her hand on his arm. 'I don't want to discuss Byron any more. And I'm sorry if I've hurt you. I really am. It's the last thing I want to do.'

'Hey, who says I'm hurt?' He tried to sound cheerful, but Danielle could see that deep down inside he was extremely saddened. 'I think I knew all along that you'd never agree to marry me. And, if it will make you feel any happier, I met a girl in Malaysia who I think I could get rather fond of. I would never have put her before you, but now that I know there's no hope maybe I'll see where things go in that direction.'

Danielle smiled at last. 'That is good. I'm pleased. I really hope things work out.'

'And for you, Danielle.' He took her hands into his. 'Life's too short to be unhappy. You ought to let Byron make up his own mind. Promise me that you'll think about telling him.'

She pulled a wry face and nodded, but knew that she wouldn't. If Tony had seen Byron today with those children he would have known there was no point.

Sleep that night was inevitably a long time in coming, and the next morning she looked out of her bedroom window at a hot blue sky—they were having a wonderful summer, and yet she'd hardly noticed it. An aeroplane droning high overhead reminded her that Byron was going to Paris today.

Had he had a sleepless night too? Was he finally convinced that they had no future together? Had she heard the last from him? The sane part of her mind wanted the answer to be yes, her heart wanted otherwise.

'I declare this shop open.'

Danielle laughed as Melissa cut the yellow ribbon they had pinned across the doorway. The last few weeks had been hectic. She had searched for and found shop premises in Stratford, she had signed the lease, she'd had the shop refitted, she had stocked it, and today it was opening with all sorts of special offers.

She planned to man this shop herself—with the help of some part-time staff. It would keep her occupied, give her no time to think, which was what she wanted right now. Tony had been a great comfort but he'd long since gone back to Malaysia, and if she dared to stop work Byron came straight back into her thoughts.

The worst times were at night. Sometimes she was so

tired that she fell to sleep immediately, but there were occasions when she lay awake and could not rid her mind of him. She wondered whether it was going to be like this for the rest of her life, or whether the pain would ease with time.

When Byron walked into her shop a couple of hours later Danielle thought she must be dreaming. Melissa had gone and she was alone, and she had actually been thinking about him. But she wasn't pleased to see him.

'What are you doing here?' she asked coldly, despite the fact that her heart had begun its usual clamour. He looked thinner and there were lines of strain on his face. She wondered whether he had been working too hard on his new project.

'Is that any way to greet a potential customer?' Dark brows rose in disapproval.

Danielle shrugged and felt slightly guilty. 'If you want to buy that's different. Please feel free to look around.' She didn't believe for one minute that he had come here with the intention of making a purchase, but he never-theless made a thorough inspection of everything—blouses, skirts, dresses, scarves, belts, jackets. And it took him so long that other customers came and went while hc was still looking.

'Can't you find what you want?' she asked at length, his presence distinctly unnerving.

'It's very difficult,' he said with a faint frown.

'Are you after anything in particular?'

'Something for a special lady.'

He had met someone else! Danielle drew in a swift, unsteady breath. She knew she ought to be pleased and yet it was like a stab in the heart, and it was all she could do to continue smiling. 'What sort of things does she like, this lady-friend of yours?'

'Nothing too fancy. I thought maybe underwear, but I see you don't stock it.'

'That's right.' Danielle's tone was sharp; she could not help it. The thought of Byron even entertaining the idea of buying such personal garments for someone he could not have long met was abhorrent. Underwear was something he had never even bought her. She chose to ignore the fact that in the days of their marriage he'd never had the money.

'Maybe a scarf,' she said, trying to think of the least personal item. 'We have some very pretty silk ones here. What colour do you think she would like?'

'Not a scarf,' he said. 'Perhaps a blouse. I like this black one. She's about your size, would you try it on for me?'

Danielle could not believe his effrontery. 'I'm sorry,' she said coolly, 'I don't have time for that.' And as if on cue two customers entered, but for the moment they just wanted to look. Danielle turned back to Byron. 'How did you find out I had opened here?'

'It's simple. I was talking business to Rod on the phone and he told me.'

But did he have to come and take a look? 'I thought you'd finally got the message.' There was a deliberate edge to her tone.

A muscle tightened in his jaw. 'Oh, I did, believe me. Well and truly.'

'So why are you here now?'

'Curiosity, I guess,' he admitted with a wry twist to his lips. 'Is this the beginning of the big time? Is Tony not as averse as John was to you becoming a career woman?'

'He doesn't mind in the least,' she told him.

Byron's eyes narrowed speculatively. 'That's good. When are you two getting married?'

'I don't think you should be asking me that question. It's none of your business.'

'So you've made no plans yet?' he deduced.

'Actually, no,' she answered.

'You're content living together?'

'A lot of people are.'

'I agree; I just didn't think you were one of them.'

'Then perhaps you don't know me as well as you thought you did.' She kept her chin high, her eyes level on his. She was giving nothing away.

'You can say that again,' he said tersely. 'I hope you'll both be very happy.'

Danielle was relieved to move away to attend to the two women, who were now interested in trying on several garments. And then, instead of returning to Byron's side, she busied herself at the counter.

Byron brought the blouse across to her. It was sheer black lace, very sexy, very provocative, and one of the most expensive items in the shop. 'I'll take this.'

Danielle glanced at the label. 'It's a size ten. Is that right?'

'Are you a ten?'

She nodded.

'Then it will fit. Except that you appear to have lost weight, Ellie.'

That makes two of us, she thought, except that it was doubtful whether his loss was because he'd been pining for her. He'd picked himself a new girlfriend pretty smart. He couldn't have been that saddened.

'Been burning the candle at both ends?'

'I've worked hard on the shop, if that's what you

mean,' she retorted, folding the blouse and popping it into a plastic carrier.

Eyebrows rose at the sharpness of her tone. 'It is not what I mean, and you know it. A little hard work never hurt anyone. But Cochran's making too many demands on you—and it shows.'

'You don't know what you're talking about,' she snapped. And, once she had given him his receipt and his change, she said, 'Excuse me; I have a customer who needs attention.'

When next she looked Byron had gone, and this time she knew that she had most definitely seen the last of him. He had accepted the inevitable. And as he now had a new lady-friend on whom he was prepared to lavish extravagant gifts she was simply a part of his past. He would not give her another thought.

What had motivated him into coming here today she did not know, unless he had been seeking final confirmation that she and Tony were a couple. Well, now he had his answer—but, in giving it to him, she had cut him out of her life for ever.

Danielle felt that she had reached rock bottom.

A day that should have proved exciting was long and tedious. Trade was brisk but customers were awkward, and when she got home she wanted to do nothing more than curl up in bed and feel sorry for herself.

But she couldn't do that because she was dining out in Birmingham with her mother and Rod. It was her mother's birthday, and Rod had said it wouldn't be right if her daughter didn't share it as well.

Rod was good for Evelyn. He had brought out a completely different side to her character. She was no longer sharply critical of others, she was tolerant, even amusing at times, and Danielle got on better with her now than she ever had.

But even so she did not enjoy the evening. The food and surroundings were in sharp contrast to the Malthouse—which ironically was only a few minutes' walk away. It was far more luxurious here, with a much more exotic menu, but actually she would have preferred the pub. Or was it because she enjoyed Byron's company more? They might argue, she might tell him to go away, but deep down inside she treasured every minute they spent together.

It was inevitable that the problems with the gallery should creep into the conversation. 'It's beginning to worry me,' Rod said. 'The whole area's had to be cordoned off in case of falling masonry. In all my experience I've never seen a crack widen so quickly. And there are others appearing. We were planning to underpin, but yesterday the inspectors were talking about pulling the whole building down.'

Danielle looked at him in horror. 'You're joking?'

'I wish I was. It could ruin the company. We'll fight it, of course. I personally think that it can be saved.'

All this because of insufficient foundations?' she queried. It was dreadful to think that the firm John had founded and built up by sheer hard work could be on the verge of ruin. It would ultimately affect her as well, but that wasn't the point at the moment.

Rod's lips thinned. 'I think Scotts took other shortcuts. It's really quite a horror story. The more I look into it, the worse it becomes.'

'John would turn in his grave if he knew.'

Rod nodded. 'It might send me into an early grave yet.'

Evelyn gasped. 'For heaven's sake, Rod, don't say that.'

He grinned and placed his hand over hers. 'I promise that I'll be here for many more years.'

It was not until they got up to leave that Danielle caught sight of Byron tucked away at a corner table. She looked twice to make sure it was him, but there was no mistake. And the woman he was with was wearing the sexy black blouse!

Somewhere at the back of her mind Danielle had had the foolish notion that he had bought the blouse for her. It was him going on about size, she supposed, and the fact that he'd wanted her to try it on.

She snapped her lips together. It really had been a stupid, stupid thought. Whoever the woman was, it fitted her perfectly. She was blonde and beautiful, and her eyes never once left Byron's face. And his first choice had been underwear! It was not difficult to imagine the sort of relationship they had.

He, too, was totally engrossed in her. He did not see Danielle or her mother or Rod get up to leave, and they had almost made it to the door before Rod happened to catch sight of him. 'Look who's there,' he said. 'The last time we spoke he was in London. Excuse me; I must have a word with him.'

Danielle and her mother waited as he crossed the room. She saw surprise register on Byron's face, and then he looked towards them, smiled briefly, and seemed to be searching for someone else. Tony, no doubt, thought Danielle grimly.

Evelyn touched her daughter's arm. 'I think he's asking us to go over.'

Danielle had seen Byron beckon too, but it was with

reluctance that she followed her mother. Her instinct had been to walk straight out of the restaurant.

'Evelyn,' said Byron at once, with a smile designed to melt icicles in the dead of winter. 'And Danielle. Please let me introduce my fiancée, Samantha Brownlee. Sam, meet Danielle and her mother.'

Danielle felt the room begin to swim, and she caught hold of the back of Byron's chair. His fiancée! *His fiancée!* It couldn't be true. He was making it up. He was paying her back because of Tony.

Her eyes slid curiously over Samantha's stunningly beautiful face. She had huge smoke-grey eyes and an unblemished skin that Danielle would die for. There wasn't a freckle in sight. The blouse looked fantastic on her, and there was total adoration in her expression when she looked at Byron.

Now Samantha said, 'How lovely to meet you, Danielle. Byron's told me so much about you. Why don't you all join us for a drink?'

'It's nice of you to ask, but I'm afraid we can't accept.'

Still reeling from the shock, Danielle heard Rod's voice from a long way away. And she was glad he was declining Samantha's offer. Byron had called her Sam. His London neighbour was Sam. Was this the same girl who looked after his roof-garden?

Rod was still speaking. 'It's Evelyn's birthday; the evening's far from over yet.'

The older woman's face brightened at the thought of more celebrations.

'Maybe Danielle could join us?' suggested Byron.

Stick your knife in a bit further, why don't you? she thought bitterly.

'Oh, yes,' said Samantha at once. 'I want to hear

about your horses. I understand you got Byron up on one. Wonders will never cease.'

'Sam is a veterinary surgeon,' informed Byron with a quiet smile. 'She's mad about animals.'

Joining them was the last thing Danielle wanted, and she felt renewed relief when Rod said, 'I wouldn't dream of leaving Danielle out. But I do want to see you Byron; maybe you could come to my office tomorrow, say about ten?'

Danielle felt Byron's eyes boring into her back as they left the restaurant, and she wondered if he knew how much like jelly her legs were. His announcement had virtually paralysed her. He had said that he'd never found anyone else to love. Had he been lying all along?

The rest of the evening passed in a trance. Why, she kept asking herself, had Byron said nothing about his engagement when he'd come to the shop? When was he going to get married? And why was she having difficulty in accepting the situation when it was the very best thing that could have happened?

The thoughts haunted her when she went to bed, and they continued to haunt what little sleep she had.

And when Byron and Samantha turned up on her doorstep the next morning Danielle thought that she must still be dreaming.

'Sam wondered if she could have a look at your horses while I'm in my meeting with Rod.' Byron watched her reaction closely.

Danielle hid her dismay, and smiled and nodded. 'Of course.' She didn't really have any choice.

'I know it's a cheek,' added Samantha, 'but I'd enjoy it much more than wandering around the shops on my own. Oh, look, there they are. Aren't they darlings?' She crossed to the fence, pulling a packet of mints from her pocket as she awaited their approach.

Why had Byron come? Danielle wondered. Was it to let her see that he had finally accepted they had no future together? Had she done such a good job of hiding her feelings and professing to love Tony that he had no idea how much he was hurting her?

'Where is loverboy this morning?' It was as if Byron had picked up on her thoughts.

Danielle raised her brows and looked at him coolly. 'At work, of course.'

'But he's not long left your bed?' His tone was dry and accusing.

'Is that any business of yours?' she queried crisply.

'It would appear not.' He turned abruptly, and called out to Sam that he was leaving.

The lingering kiss he gave the other girl could not have hurt Danielle more had he plucked her heart out with his bare hands. It almost killed her to stand and watch them, and she felt no better after he had gone.

'I did try to tell Byron that we should have phoned first,' said Samantha, following Danielle into the house. 'But he was sure you wouldn't mind. I hope you didn't have any plans for this morning?'

'Nothing in particular.' Fortunately, or perhaps unfortunately, Danielle had asked one of her part-time ladies to look after the shop because she had known that she wouldn't be able to concentrate after last night's events. And Byron must have assumed that she employed someone to run it—the same way Melissa ran her Birmingham one—otherwise why would he have expected to find her in? He'd come almost eighteen miles out of his way, for goodness' sake!

'Byron has told me so much about you.'

'All good, I hope?' enquired Danielle with a faint smile.

Samantha was much taller than she had thought, naturally graceful, very pleasant and open and friendly, and much as Danielle wanted to dislike her she found it impossible. A huge diamond glittered on the third finger of her left hand, and Danielle could not keep her eyes off it. When she had become engaged to Byron he had not even been able to afford a ring.

'But of course,' said Samantha. 'First loves are always special, don't you think?'

So she even knew they had been married before! Did she also know that he had been chasing her again recently? 'You certainly never forget them,' agreed Danielle.

'I remember my first love.' Samantha looked wistful. 'I didn't marry him, but I would have liked to.'

'He didn't love you?'

Samantha shook her head. 'Unfortunately, no.'

But now she was in love again. She had the glow that all women in love had. That Danielle's own mother had. But which was denied herself because she was forced to keep her love hidden!

'Would you like a cup of tea?' She was determined to push such thoughts out of her mind.

'Please, if it's no trouble. It seems hours since we had breakfast.'

Danielle filled the kettle. 'Have you known Byron long?'

Samantha smiled, as though happy to be talking about him. 'Three years. We're actually neighbours.'

'Yes, I rather gathered that. Don't you look after his roof-garden?'

Samantha smiled. 'He's mentioned me?' She looked

delighted. 'Yes, I do that whenever he's away—which is quite often.'

'And you don't mind?'

'It's a pleasure. All I have is a little balcony. I love gardens. I love being outdoors.'

That wasn't what Danielle had meant. She wanted to know whether Samantha objected to him being away from home so much. 'Who's looking after the plants now?'

'My flatmate. I had a few days' holiday due, and Byron phoned yesterday morning and suggested I come up to Birmingham and spend them with him. He's quite a man, isn't he? I can't imagine why you two guys ever split up.'

'These things happen,' said Danielle with what she hoped was a careless shrug.

'Actually—' and Samantha said it without rancour '—I'd always gained the impression that he was still in love with you, that there would never be anyone else. I lived in hope because I'm desperately in love with him, but I never dreamt he would ever return it.' A beautiful smile lit up her whole face. 'I couldn't believe my good fortune when he produced this ring last night and asked me to marry him. Oh, Danielle, I'm the happiest girl in the world.'

CHAPTER TEN

'IT LOOKS as though you and I have both hit the jackpot.'

Byron frowned at Rod. 'What are you talking about?' As far as he was concerned the whole gallery project was a disaster. And although he had been cleared of any blame, no one could stop the rumours that were beginning to circulate. If they were believed it could be the beginning of the end of his career.

'Finding the right woman to spend the rest of our lives with.'

'Oh, that.' His engagement was the furthest thought from his mind.

'Samantha's very beautiful.'

Byron nodded.

'How many years has it been since you split up with Danielle?'

'Almost ten,' he answered abruptly. Discussing his personal affairs wasn't why he was here.

'A long time to be alone,' said Rod. 'It's been eight years since my wife died. Do you know, since meeting Eve I feel like a new man again? Is that how you feel?'

Byron wished he wouldn't keep asking these questions. 'I guess I do,' he said, more to keep Rod happy than because it was true. He was fond of Samantha and he had no doubt that his marriage to her would be a happy one—*if* he ever went through with it. He still held out a faint hope that... He dashed the thought away. Danielle was no longer available to him; he had to remember that.

When Rod finally got to the business in hand and told Byron about the possibility of the gallery being pulled down, he could have wept. According to the private detective he had hired, John Smith must have had some idea of what was going on. He'd been asking lots of questions, getting a lot of people's backs up, and it was about that time the accident had happened!

He questioned Rod about it again, and this time, reluctantly, after much prompting, the other man admitted that he had thought there was more to John's death than had been reported.

'I went to the police, but they wouldn't listen. They said there was no reason to think there had been foul play. I guess I should have been more insistent, and I would have been if...' He suddenly dropped his head in his hands.

Byron did not press the issue because he could see that Rod was upset, but he was most certainly not going to rest until he had got to the bottom of it.

And when he had concrete evidence, when he had found the guy who had been the cause of John's death—he was proving to be very elusive—he would go to the police. He would not allow himself to be fobbed off the way Rod had.

Rod seemed almost to be scared of them. Perhaps he'd once been in trouble. A driving offence, maybe? Something trivial, something that made him afraid.

And he might also say something to Danielle, Byron decided. He would wait and see; he would play it by ear. He did not want to disturb her unduly, although he still thought that she ought to know the truth.

On his way to pick up Samantha, Byron wondered how the two women had got on. His announcement last night had come as a tremendous shock to Danielle. So much so that she had been forced to take hold of his chair to steady herself. She had probably thought he wouldn't notice, but he had. There was not one thing that he missed where Danielle was concerned.

It had been unfair of him to foist Samantha on her today, but it had been Sam's own idea, and as far as he was concerned it had given him one more chance to see Danielle. He knew every inch of her face and her body by memory, he would never forget them, and even though she was now lost to him for ever he had not wanted to miss another opportunity to see her, to talk to her, to breathe in the sweet, heady excitement of her.

When he'd dropped Samantha off she had looked as though she'd hardly slept, and he would have liked to think that it was because of his shock engagement. But he knew the likely truth was that that swine Tony had kept her awake with another night of lovemaking.

His lips were grim as he pulled his car onto the driveway. He automatically looked across to the paddock and saw that both the horses were out. And when he rang the bell no one answered. He walked round to the back of the house and made himself comfortable on Danielle's swinging hammock to await their return.

He'd had a restless night, thinking about Danielle—and the future he'd mapped out for himself—and before he knew it he was asleep.

'Byron.'

He'd been dreaming about Danielle, dreaming that they were getting married again, but when he opened his eyes it was Samantha touching his shoulder, Samantha calling his name. He looked beyond her, but Danielle was nowhere in sight.

'Wake up, sleepyhead,' she said with a smile and a light kiss.

He sat up. 'What time is it?'

'Lunchtime. Danielle's invited us to stay. She's a really nice person, Byron. I'm glad I've met her.'

He wondered what Danielle thought of Sam, but knew he would never dare to ask. Despite her shock she would be pleased for him, pleased that he had found someone else, because it meant that he would no longer be a nuisance to her.

Danielle stared sightlessly out of the kitchen window. The news that Byron had asked Samantha to marry him only last night had devastated her. His visit to the shop must have been a last-ditch attempt to patch things up between them. And she had been so successful in her mission to get rid of him that he'd got himself engaged to another girl.

How was she going to put on a brave face over lunch? She wanted to disappear, she wanted to sink down into a hole in the ground. Why she had suggested they stay, she did not know—except that she had got on so well with Samantha that it had seemed a natural thing to do.

Sam was a wonderful person, so friendly and open. No airs or graces, no awkwardness over Byron. Sam accepted that Danielle had once been his wife, she wasn't jealous or spiteful or anything like that, and saw no reason why they couldn't be friends.

And the odd thing was, Danielle couldn't even be jealous of Sam. She found herself hoping that the two of them would be happy together. It was what Byron deserved after so many years being on his own. Whether Samantha was second best or whether he really did love her, she would never know. She did know, though—and thinking about it brought tears to her eyes—that he'd discussed having children with Samantha. Sam had been full of it when she'd told Danielle.

'Why didn't you two ever have any?' she had asked in her forthright manner.

Danielle had shrugged. 'We were young; we were in no hurry.' She was glad Byron hadn't told Sam about her miscarriage.

Over lunch Danielle kept a smile pinned to her lips, and refused to let Byron see by even the flicker of an eyelash that it was killing her, sitting here with the two of them.

Samantha, unaware of any tension, babbled on about the horses and their ride. 'I wish I lived in the country,' she said, 'instead of penned up in London. What do you think, Byron? Could we move when we get married? I could even open my own veterinary surgery. That would be wonderful.' Her soft grey eyes were alight with enthusiasm.

'We'll have to think about it,' he said. 'London's a perfect base for me.'

Samantha nodded. 'You're right, of course. But when we have children it won't be fair to bring them up in the city, especially not in your penthouse, big as it is.'

'We'll see about that when the time comes.'

Danielle closed her eyes in a futile attempt to shut out this conversation. Life was so unfair. *So grossly unfair.* Why had this happened to her? Why should Sam be able to have children when she couldn't? Why should Sam provide Byron with the family he yearned for when it was herself he loved and her children he really wanted? When she loved him more than life itself? It was total injustice.

As she fought back tears she was faintly conscious of Sam saying, 'We could even find somewhere near here so that we could see Danielle occasionally. We got on so well together this morning that I should hate never to see her again. What do you think, Danielle? Oh, is something wrong?'

Danielle covered her face with her hands, not wanting either of them to see how upset she was, especially Byron. 'I—I don't feel well,' she said in a voice choked with emotion. 'Excuse me.' And she ran from the room.

'Ellie?' Byron was immediately full of concern.

She ignored him and raced up the stairs, shot into her bedroom and locked the door. Tears fell even before she threw herself on the bed.

'Ellie, open the door.'

She didn't even hear Byron's anxious voice. This was the worst scenario she could ever have imagined. Why did they have to talk like this in front of her? Why did they have to make their plans? Why couldn't they wait until they were alone? Didn't they know it tortured her?

'Ellie!' A loud knock accompanied his commanding voice.

This time she heard and gave an inward groan. 'Go away.' The last thing she wanted was Byron seeing her like this. And as though he might walk in at any moment she rushed across to her bathroom and locked that door as well.

She sat down on the lavatory seat and dropped her head in her hands. She really did feel ill now. All she wanted was for them to go away and leave her alone, to disappear out of her life for ever. Byron and his fiancée, Byron and the woman who was going to bear his babies, be the mother of his children. Children! She could not contain her wail of misery.

'Danielle, I demand that you open this door immediately. If you don't, I will break it down.'

Byron's voice reached her loud and clear, and she heard Sam's quieter tones as she spoke to him. They must think she was crazy, shooting off and locking herself in. If she'd really been ill would she have done that? Of course not. If only they would go. But they wouldn't, not until they had assured themselves that she was all right.

'Danielle.' It was Samantha this time. 'We're very worried about you. Was it the prawns? Do you want us to call a doctor?'

If only it were something that simple. If only there were a cure for a broken heart. She mopped her face on a towel and unlocked the bathroom door. 'No. I'll be out in a minute.' She marvelled at how steady her voice sounded.

'Can we help?'

'No, Sam, it's all right. Go and finish your lunch.'

'How the hell do you expect us to do that when you're in there feeling sick?' thundered Byron. 'Open the damn door.'

'I will in a minute,' she repeated, beginning to feel angry herself now. 'Can't you give me some breathing space?'

She heard Sam say something to Byron and him answering her back. And then he said impatiently, 'This is a ridiculous situation, but I'll give you ten minutes. If you're not back down by then, be prepared to have your door smashed.'

In her mind's eye Danielle saw them waiting for some sort of response from her, but when none was forthcoming they reluctantly left. She heard their soft footfalls on the stairs.

She could understand their concern—she would have felt the same herself had the positions been reversed—

but there was not a thing she could do about it. Something had snapped inside her head when she'd heard them discussing their future plans—a future which involved the man she loved but not herself! A future which included the one thing she could never have.

A fresh flood of tears streamed down her cheeks and she thought they would never stop. She had to use every ounce of self-control, splashing her face repeatedly with cold water to get rid of her red eyes and blotchy skin. When she left the bedroom her ten minutes were up.

Byron was waiting at the bottom of the stairs; she wondered if he had been there all the time. He watched her descend, his arms akimbo, silvery grey eyes raking her face.

She stopped on the last step.

'Are you feeling better?' he asked.

Danielle nodded, unwilling to trust her voice.

'What was wrong?'

She stuck to her earlier excuse. 'I felt nauseous.'

'You sounded as though you were crying,' he accused. 'Was it the thought of us coming to live near you? Did you think we might intrude on your privacy? Upset the little love-nest you're busy building with loverboy Cochran? You needn't worry,' he sneered. 'I've persuaded Sam it would be a bad idea. The thought abhors me too, if you want the truth.'

He didn't want to see her ever again, not even as a friend! The thought poleaxed her, but from somewhere she dragged up some pride. 'I'm glad the feeling's mutual.' And she was pleased at the cool strength of her voice.

'If it's all right with you, I think Sam and I will go now,' he said, his tone equally chilly. 'We've intruded enough on your time.'

She inclined her head. 'Very well. And may I congratulate you on your engagement? Sam's a nice girl; I'm sure you'll be very happy with her.' How she said the words Danielle did not know. Her heart was breaking, she was weeping inside, but there was a brave smile on her face.

'I'm sure I will be,' he responded. 'May I return the felicitation?'

'Thank you,' she said, and as she descended the last step she was so close to Byron that she could feel the heat of his body more than usual, smell the savage, special, male odour of him more than usual. Every sense was intensified. She could hear his laboured breathing, see every pore, the faint sheen of perspiration, almost taste him.

She wanted to put her hands out and touch him for one last time, she wanted to feel his arms about her, she wanted to feel his lips on hers, drink the sweet nectar of life from his mouth, and she sensed that he was fighting the same inner battle. Was that why his breathing was uneven? Why he was sweating.

She was never to know for sure because Samantha joined them at that critical moment. 'Danielle, you're feeling better? I've cleared away and washed up for you; I knew you wouldn't feel like doing it.'

'You're very kind,' said Danielle, reluctantly breaking eye contact with Byron.

'You still look pale.'

'I've told Danielle we're leaving,' Byron informed his fiancée tersely.

Samantha frowned. 'Do you really think we should? Will you be all right, Danielle?'

Danielle nodded. 'I'm fine again now. I do apologise; I don't know what came over me.'

'If you're sure?' Samantha still looked anxious.

'Hasn't she said she's sure?' growled Byron.

Samantha raised her fine, pale brows and said in a loud whisper to Danielle, 'What's wrong with him?'

Danielle shrugged.

'There's nothing wrong except that I think we've outstayed our welcome,' he grated. 'Come along, Sam.'

Clearly puzzled, Samantha gave Danielle a big hug. 'I hope we see each other soon,' she said with genuine affection. 'And if ever you're in London do drop in. You have Byron's address?'

Byron gave Danielle no chance to answer. 'Goodbye,' he said.

And never had one word sounded so final.

In the days that followed Danielle's whole life felt empty. She existed; she went on from day to day, living, working, doing whatever she had to do. But it had no meaning.

She wondered, belatedly, whether Tony was right and she should have told Byron what had happened to her, given him the chance to make his own decision. Even if he had walked away it would have been no harder than it was now, and at least he would have known.

She wrote to Tony, telling him about Byron and Samantha, making light of it, declaring that it was the best thing that could have happened, and he immediately phoned her and said she was a fool and that it was still not too late to do something about it. But Danielle knew that she never would. She had lost her opportunity.

A week later at Evelyn's house her mother announced over lunch that she and Rod were getting married. All the time Danielle was offering congratulations her heart felt as heavy as lead. Another wedding. Another reason for her to feel dejected. She had heard only yesterday from a highly excited friend that she was pregnant for the second time, and it had brought her own loss back with a vengeance. Every time she saw someone with a baby she thought of her own little Lucy.

'We've fixed the date for four weeks tomorrow,' said Evelyn as she ladled a second helping of potatoes on to Danielle's plate. 'And mind you eat these; you're getting far too thin. I know it doesn't give me much time to organise things, but Rod saw no reason why we should wait.'

'Nor do I,' said Danielle. 'What are you going to wear?'

There followed a lengthy discussion about suitable clothes. And when that was exhausted, when they had agreed to go on a shopping spree the very next day, Evelyn said, 'I was surprised to hear Byron say he was engaged. I didn't know he had a girlfriend. You must be very relieved, Danielle.'

'Relieved?' she asked with a frown.

Her mother tutted. 'Because it will get him off your back.'

'He's never been on my back,' Danielle declared fiercely. She did not want to discuss Byron; she had been praying her mother wouldn't bring him into the conversation. She supposed it had been too much to hope. If her parent hadn't been so full of her own wedding plans, Byron's engagement would have been the first thing on her agenda.

'His fiancée looks a nice girl. And Byron has changed too. He's more of a gentleman these days, much nicer than he used to be.'

How big of her mother to admit it, thought Danielle,

though she suspected it was only because he was now safely committed to someone else.

'Have they fixed a date for their wedding yet?'

'I've no idea,' said Danielle, and the horrible thought struck her that she might be invited! It was something she could never go through. It would be purgatory, sheer hell, the worst form of punishment imaginable.

She had a sudden urge to flee the country, to do anything to get out of going to Byron's wedding. Obviously she couldn't go until after her mother and Rod got married, but there would be nothing to stop her then. She wouldn't feel compelled to be on hand in case her mother needed her, as she had felt in the past.

In the days that followed Danielle thought more and more about going away, and became convinced that it was the right thing to do. Especially when she could not cleanse her mind of either Byron or Samantha. She had this image of a smiling, happy, glowing Samantha. Samantha declaring her love for Byron. Samantha wearing the sexy black blouse.

Sam had told her about the blouse when they'd gone on their ride. 'Wasn't it perfectly sweet of him? When he told me where we were going to eat I wailed that I had nothing to wear. I'd packed so quickly that I hadn't put in anything dressy. He said not to worry, that he had something in his wardrobe that would fit. How he came to have it I don't know, and I didn't dare ask. But it was brand-new, and it's totally adorable. I love it.'

Danielle had said nothing—not that he'd bought it from her shop, not that he'd asked her to try it on for him. All she had been able to think about was the fact that initially he had been going to buy underwear!

She attended another board meeting, and much to her relief Byron was not invited. JBS were fighting to save the gallery. They were of the opinion that a good building firm could still do the necessary work. And afterwards Rod took Danielle into his office. 'Have you heard when Byron's wedding is?'

Danielle's heart took off at a gallop. 'No, I haven't. When?' Not soon, please not soon—not before she had made her plans.

'No, I don't mean I know,' he said quickly, 'I just wondered if you did? Eve and I would naturally like to buy them a present, and I thought that if it was while your mother and I are away—I've booked us on a three-month cruise, but I haven't told her about it yet,' he added with a confidential grin, 'I would entrust it to you to give to them. And don't worry about things here because Gordon is going to look after everything in my absence.'

Gordon Steele was the sales director and a very able man, and Danielle knew he had the company's interests at heart. That wasn't what bothered her at this moment.

'I would give your present to them,' she said slowly, 'but the truth is, Rod, that I might not be here when they get married. I'm thinking of going abroad myself.' She hadn't made any firm plans yet, but she had definitely made up her mind.

'I'm going to let my house—' she was improvising quickly now '—Melissa is going to look after my shops, and I'm going to tour America for a year. John has relatives in Aspen. They own a ranch, and are always asking me to visit.' Which was true. 'I shall probably spend quite a bit of time with them.'

His eyes widened. 'When did you plan all this? Does your mother know?'

Danielle shook her head.

'Were you going to tell her before the wedding?'

She grimaced. 'Actually, no. But if you're going to be away for three months then I'll have to.'

'She won't be happy.'

'I know,' Danielle agreed. 'That's why I didn't want to say anything before you got married. I didn't want to spoil her pleasure. I've never seen her this happy in a long time, Rod. But this is something that I've wanted to do for ages.' The lies seemed to slip easily off her tongue.

'Since John died perhaps?' he asked, suddenly understanding.

She was quick to accept his reasoning. 'Yes, as a matter of fact. But I haven't been able to because I didn't want to leave my mother on her own. Now that she has you, there's nothing to stop me.'

'Maybe you'll get homesick long before your twelve months are up,' he suggested hopefully.

She smiled. 'Maybe.'

'And I think it might be best if I'm there when you tell your mother.'

Danielle nodded. She had been thinking the same thing herself.

The next few weeks were hectic. Apart from helping her mother organise her wedding, she had her own travel arrangements to take care of. There was her house to think about, and the horses would have to go out on loan. She did not fancy leaving the building empty for twelve months, but nor did she like the idea of a complete stranger living there.

When Melissa said that her elder sister, Fiona, was being forced to leave her flat at the end of the month because her lease wasn't being renewed—probably because her landlord wanted it for his mistress, Melissa had declared spitefully—Danielle knew that she had found the ideal tenant. Fiona was a keen horsewoman as well, which meant that Sandor and Morgan would also be taken care of.

Which left her shops. She had begun to wish that she had never opened her second one in Stratford. It had seemed like a good idea, until suddenly she had no time for it. It was beginning to be a real headache.

Melissa came to the rescue again. She had a new, wealthy boyfriend who ran a wholesale clothing company with whom Danielle did business. It was how they had met.

'Adrian says it's about time I had a shop or two of my own,' she told Danielle. 'Would you be interested in selling?'

Would she? The deal was struck, and all in all Danielle had little time to think about Byron and Samantha. When she did, usually in her bed at night, the pain was unbearable, and she knew that she was doing the right thing in being out of the country when they got married.

Her mother's wedding day went like a dream. The bride was radiant, the groom couldn't stop grinning, and Evelyn had even forgiven Danielle for the fact that she was going to spend a year in America.

Byron and Samantha had been invited, but to Danielle's intense relief they had said they couldn't come, that business commitments wouldn't allow it. Whether it was the truth she didn't know, but it meant that she could breathe easy.

Waving her mother and new stepfather off on their honeymoon, Danielle was very much aware that in a further two days' time she would be leaving England herself. In fact she was quite looking forward to it. She had never been to America before, and John's relatives had said she could stay with them for as long as she liked.

It was on her last night in England as she sat reading the evening newspaper that one paragraph jumped out at her, made her forget that she had been about to go to bed, made her shoot out of her seat and run for her car keys and her jacket.

CHAPTER ELEVEN

DANIELLE drove to the hospital like a woman possessed, and she could not help thinking how she had very nearly cancelled her evening newspaper. If she had, she would never have read that Byron was fighting for his life. She would have flown to America and not known. It didn't bear thinking about.

Car horns blared as she veered in and out of traffic with no thought for her own safety. It was almost midnight; she could not think where all the cars were going, but she had to be there, she had to see him, speak to him. What if he died without ever knowing that she still loved him? Without knowing about baby Lucy? Tears blurred her vision and she dashed them away with the back of her hand.

She screeched into the hospital carpark, raced into Reception, found out where Byron was, and ran along corridors, receiving several disapproving looks as she did so.

She pushed open the door and came to an abrupt halt. It was like looking at John all over again. The same shaved head, the same tubes and wires connected to him. The same scary pieces of machinery that were doing God knew what. The same stern-faced nurse sitting at his bedside.

And John had died!

Every ounce of blood drained from her face and she took an unsteady step forward.

'Who are you?' asked the nurse in her prim, hushed voice.

'I'm Byron's ex-wife. Oh, Lord, is he going to die?' Tears filled her eyes again and she looked from the nurse to Byron, and she wanted to rush over to him, hold him, talk to him, open her heart to him. But he wouldn't hear because he was unconscious. Or was he just asleep? She didn't know.

All she knew was that some crumbling masonry from the gallery had fallen on him. It was like history repeating itself. She could remember clearly the last time she'd been here—the pain, the worry, the fear. And John hadn't made it. He'd never regained consciousness. He'd quietly slipped away while she'd sat holding his hand.

God, please don't let it happen to Byron, she prayed. Because if Byron died her pain would be intensified a thousandfold. It would be too much to bear. She would want to die too.

'We're doing everything we can for him,' the nurse told her.

Which was what they always said. 'Is he unconscious?'

For the first time the nurse smiled. 'Not any more. He came round about an hour ago. He's asleep now.'

'What injuries does he have?'

'A fractured skull, and the surgeon has operated to relieve pressure on the brain. He'll probably sleep for hours. If I were you I'd come back tomorrow.'

But I'm flying to America tomorrow. The words were never said because Danielle knew that she would not go, not while Byron was fighting for his life. 'Couldn't I sit a while? No one told me; I read it in the paper. I—' Her voice broke and tears rolled unchecked down her cheeks.

No one had thought to tell her. No one knew how much she cared.

'Maybe for a few minutes,' said the nurse kindly. 'In fact I could do with a break. Press the bell if there's any change. Anything, you understand?'

Danielle swallowed and nodded and groped in her pocket for a handkerchief. When the nurse had gone, she sat down beside Byron and very gently, very, very gently, put her hand over his where it lay on the covers.

'Byron. Oh, Byron.' Her words were the faintest whisper. 'I love you so much. Please don't die. There's so much I have to say to you. So much I should have said before.'

She studied every inch of his face, once so warm and vital and full of life, now so pale and still. He didn't even look as though he was breathing; only the faint rise and fall of his chest beneath the sheets told her. She found herself constantly watching for it, even though she knew that the monitors were keeping a much closer watch than she ever could.

His thick lashes stood out starkly against the whiteness of his skin, two dark crescents fanning bruised eye sockets. She wanted to kiss them. She wanted to kiss his cheeks, his mouth. She wanted to slide in bed beside him, warm him with her body, breathe her life into him so that he got better quickly.

He was going to get better, the nurse had said. And she was going to hang onto that thought. At least he had regained consciousness, which was more than John had, and even if he had a long fight in front of him then she would be with him every inch of the way.

His fiancée was forgotten. This was her Byron, the man she loved, the man she had always loved right from the day he had shoved his collecting bucket under her nose. And this was her rightful place.

She closed her eyes for a few seconds, and then jerked them open when she felt his hand move beneath hers, a faint lifting of his fingers, as though he wanted to do more but the weight of her hand was holding him down.

'Byron,' she said in a much louder whisper. 'It's me, Danielle. Are you awake? Can you hear me?'

Heavy eyelids slowly opened, slate-grey eyes tried to focus. 'Ellie? My Ellie?'

It was the way he said 'My Ellie' that caused fresh tears, brought a sudden lump to her throat. 'Yes,' she whispered fervently. 'It's me.' Forgotten was her promise to ring for the nurse. This was her and Byron. No one else existed in the whole wide world.

'I love you, Ellie.'

Her face crumpled. She wanted to break down and cry her heart out. He had said it so naturally, as he used to when they'd first met, when they'd married. 'I love you, Ellie, and I always will'. So many times he had said that. 'You're the only girl in the world for me'.

And she had walked out on him! She had broken his heart. But no more. She was going to tell him exactly why she had done it. She was going to declare her love. She was leaving nothing unspoken. Life was too short for that.

'And I love you, Byron.' It was a firm declaration of the truth, spoken from her heart. 'I love you so very much.'

He tried to smile, and he lifted his hand and touched her face. But Danielle could see the effort it took and she held his hand steady, pressing her lips to his palm, to his fingers, at the same time locking her eyes with his.

She saw pain, but she also saw the full strength of his love. 'I'm worried about you,' she said.

His eyes closed for an instant and then opened again. 'Don't be worried.' It was an effort for him to speak. 'I—I—' His hand went limp and heavy in hers and he was asleep again.

The nurse returned. Danielle did not tell her that he had woken; she savoured the precious moments instead. Whether he would ever remember them she did not know, but he had said that he loved her, and she had finally admitted that she loved him too. If he didn't make it, at least she had told him. She felt faintly better.

When the nurse suggested she go home Danielle got herself a cup of vending-machine coffee instead. She was not leaving until she knew whether Byron was going to be all right.

A couple of hours and several polystyrene cups of coffee later she returned to his room. He was alone. She crept in and settled herself in the chair beside him. His hands were tucked beneath the sheets this time; everything was neat and orderly. But she thought there was more colour in his face. Or was it wishful thinking?

She stroked the backs of her fingers against his cheek, and then because that was not enough she stood up and leaned over him and touched her lips to his.

Byron made a low noise in the back of his throat, a satisfied noise, as though he knew what she was doing and he was enjoying it. She pressed her lips even closer and felt a faint response. 'Are you awake?' she whispered against his mouth.

'I'm being kissed by an angel,' he said.

Again this was something he had used to say to her. It gave her a lovely warm feeling, yet at the same time she could not help wondering whether Byron had lost his immediate memory. Whether he had forgotten their divorce, remembered only the good times. It would be wonderful in the short term, but when his memory came back the agony would start all over again.

She sat back in the chair, and when he felt her move he opened his eyes and looked at her with a faint frown, dragging his dark brows together. 'Am I dreaming?' he asked.

Danielle shook her head, smiling gently. 'It's really me.'

'What am I doing here?'

'You had an accident.'

A further frown as he struggled to remember. 'What sort of an accident?'

'I don't think you should be talking about it,' she said.

He gave a weary smile and, pulling his hand out from beneath the covers, he reached for hers. 'So long as you're here, that's all that matters.'

For the first time since she had arrived, Danielle thought about Samantha. But if he couldn't remember then she wouldn't mention her—not yet, anyway. 'Nothing would keep me away,' she said, her eyes shining with love.

'I love you, Ellie, so very, very much.'

She held his hand between both of hers, never wanting to let him go, not ever again. 'I know, Byron, and I love you too, with all my heart.'

'Ellie.'

'Yes?'

'Kiss me again.'

She needed no second bidding.

Neither of them saw Samantha standing in the doorway.

*   *   *

Dawn was breaking when Danielle drove slowly home, careful now, considerate, obeying the rules of the road. She even managed to hum to herself. She knew that Byron had a long way to go, but he was going to get better. He had said that himself. He had said that a little thing like a bump on the head was not going to separate him from her.

She treasured these thoughts. She knew that when his full memory returned, when he remembered Tony and Samantha, then these few hours of pleasure would be over, but for the moment they lifted her spirits.

Presumably someone had told Samantha? Presumably his fiancée had already been to see him and would be back again soon? There was a very strong possibility that she would never have Byron to herself again.

If only she could have stayed longer, snatched a few hours more with the man she loved. But the nurse had come back and grimly ordered her out.

And Byron had looked tired. In fact, when she'd turned back in the doorway, he'd already been asleep. She had promised she would return, and she would, but deep down inside she knew that it would be different. Those few minutes of closeness, when his memory had fooled him, would never be repeated.

Indeed when she visited him later, after having managed a couple of hours' sleep herself, after cancelling her flight and phoning John's relatives, Samantha was already there.

Danielle thought there was an incredible sadness in Byron's eyes as she bent to give him a brief kiss on the cheek. It was nothing like yesterday's kiss. It was the sort she would give a brother or a close friend. Was he thinking the same? Or was it the pain in his head that caused the sorrow?

'I'm glad you've come,' he said, but that was all.

Sam, too, looked at her strangely, perhaps even sympathetically. Or was it her imagination working overtime?

'Oh, Danielle,' Samantha said at once, 'I'm glad you're here as well. Isn't it truly awful? Poor Byron. I nearly died yesterday when the hospital phoned. Who told you? I was going to ring you myself this morning.'

'I saw it in the paper,' said Danielle.

'Oh, poor you,' cried Samantha at once, and her concern was genuine. 'What a dreadful way to find out. Oh, Lord, I wish I'd phoned you yesterday now. I'm so sorry, I wasn't thinking straight, I—'

'Isn't anyone going to talk to me?'

They both stopped and looked guiltily at Byron. 'Sorry,' they said in unison, and then both began talking at once.

Danielle discovered that Byron now remembered everything. 'It was a stupid thing to do,' he admitted. 'I know I shouldn't have been so near, but I wanted a closer look. I was there no more than a minute.'

'A minute which almost proved fatal,' Samantha reproved, though she was careful to be gentle. 'They wouldn't have cordoned the gallery off if it wasn't dangerous.'

But Danielle knew how he felt. She knew how much any of the buildings he had designed meant to him. They were his babies—the ones she couldn't give him! He conceived them, they grew and developed inside him and were finally born. And if one of them was dying, like the gallery, then he had to be there at the end.

They weren't allowed to stay long for fear of tiring Byron. Samantha left first, saying to Danielle, 'I need to go to the Ladies'. You have a minute with Byron and

I'll see you outside. Perhaps we could have a coffee together somewhere?'

Danielle nodded, but the moment she and Byron were alone she was terrified. They had opened their hearts yesterday, and now today his fiancée stood between them.

'Give me your hand.'

Slowly she did as he asked, but she was trembling.

'I know what we said last night,' Byron said softly, 'and I meant every word. But I also realise that you were only humouring me, saying what you thought I wanted to hear. I haven't forgotten Tony.'

Danielle opened her mouth to speak, but he stopped her. 'And there's Sam to consider, of course. It all came back to me the minute she walked in.'

Tears formed but she refused to let them fall. So he was still going to marry Sam. The lump in her throat got bigger. It became impossible to speak. She simply looked at him, her blue eyes wide and luminous—and incredibly sad.

'I think you'd better go,' he said.

'Byron is awesomely strong, don't you think?' Samantha nibbled a biscuit and looked thoughtfully at Danielle.

They had found a side-street café and were sitting in the bow-fronted window where they could watch the passers-by.

'He's certainly recovering quickly,' Danielle agreed.

'When I first saw him I wasn't sure he'd make it. And now he's sitting up and behaving as though hardly anything has happened.'

'That wasn't quite what I meant,' said Samantha. 'I meant strength of character. There's not much that sets him back, is there?'

'I suppose not,' said Danielle, frowning, wondering what was on the other woman's mind.

'He must have taken plenty of hard knocks in his life, but he picks himself up, dusts himself down, and gets on with it, doesn't he?'

'He's certainly not one to dwell on things,' she agreed.

'So if I break off our engagement he won't go to pieces?'

'Sam!' exclaimed Danielle. 'What are you saying? I thought you were madly in love with him.'

'I am.'

'So why are you talking like this?'

'Because you love him more, and he loves you, Danielle. Don't try to deny it because I know.'

Danielle felt instant shock, and she quite firmly shook her head. 'You're wrong, Sam. There can never be anything between Byron and me.'

Samantha looked at her long and hard. She took a sip from her coffee cup and put it down. Then she leaned her arms on the table and looked directly at Danielle. 'When I visited Byron last night they wouldn't let me stay. They said I was wasting my time, that he would sleep for hours. They advised me to get some sleep myself.

'But I couldn't. I paced my hotel room for Lord knows how long, and in the end I went back to the hospital. I saw you with him. I saw how you reacted to each other. I heard what you both said. And I knew then that Byron was lost to me—if I ever had him.'

Danielle didn't know what to say. She was deeply embarrassed for one thing, and could hardly believe that Sam was being so noble. 'You don't know the whole story,' she said at length.

'Then why don't you tell me?' suggested Samantha softly. Her smoke-grey eyes held no ill feeling; she truly wanted to know why the two of them had lived apart for so many years when they still cared for each other.

She must have been stunned when she overheard their declarations of love, thought Danielle, and she would have given anything to replay that scene all over again. This poor, poor girl was being so magnanimous when her own heart must be breaking. If anything, Sam was the strong one.

'What made you walk out on your marriage?' prompted Samantha when Danielle remained silent.

Not knowing whether she was doing the right thing, loading her guilt onto Sam, Danielle began hesitantly, but soon she was spilling out the whole story, and with it came the inevitable tears.

'And you've never told Byron any of this?' Samantha asked when she had finished.

Danielle shook her head. 'I couldn't. And I thought I was completely over him,' she said with a wry twist to her lips. 'Until I bumped into him again.' She dabbed her streaming eyes with a serviette.

'Did you know he still loved you?'

'Yes,' said Danielle quietly. 'He told me.'

'But you denied your own love because of your infertility?'

'Yes.' Her voice was even fainter.

'Do you think you were being fair on Byron?'

'Of course I was,' Danielle insisted. 'He wants children, Sam, you know that. I want you to push everything I have told you right out of your mind, go ahead and marry him and give him the family he wants, which he deserves. I am no good to him, Sam. Can't you understand that?'

She turned her head away, mopping her face again, glad the little café was deserted. She ought not to have told Sam. It was the wrong thing to have done. Oh, God, she prayed, just whisk me away from here, take me anywhere, but get me out of this difficult situation.

Of course, He didn't.

'What I can understand is that you're very emotional at this moment,' said Samantha, with so much concern and warmth in her voice that it induced a further flood of tears. 'But I also think that you underestimate Byron. I think you should at least let him make the decision.'

'You mean tell him?' Danielle's wide, moist eyes looked at Samantha in disbelief.

'I mean exactly that.'

Danielle shook her head. 'I can't; I couldn't. It wouldn't be right. I mean, I have thought of it, but it would put him in a difficult situation. It's best that things stay as they are. And *you're* not to tell him. You have to promise me that, Sam.'

It took a long time for Samantha to answer. 'Very well, I'll say nothing, but I think you're a fool, Danielle. A nice one,' she added with a sympathetic smile.

'Will you also promise not to break off your engagement?'

This time there was no hesitation. 'I can't do that. I will choose my time carefully, that's all I can say, but it would be wrong to let him go through with it when he's not in love with me.'

'You can't be sure of that.'

'I'm second best,' admitted Samantha ruefully. 'What I want to know is what happened between you two to make him suddenly propose to me? It was shock enough when he rang and asked me to spend a few days with him in Birmingham, but when he asked me to marry him, well—I nearly had to be carried out on a stretcher.

'It was my dream come true, and yet at the same time I couldn't believe that he'd suddenly decided that he loved me. There had to be more to it than that. So I'm asking you, what happened?'

Danielle sighed. 'I let him think that Tony had moved in with me. You know about Tony?'

Samantha nodded. 'Some. I take it you don't love him?'

'Only as a friend. Tony wanted more but I couldn't give it to him, and he only stayed with me for a few days because he had nowhere else to go. But Byron saw him when he'd just come out of the shower and drew his own conclusions. It was the get-out I was looking for. I let him think the worst.' She pulled a wry face. 'It seemed like a good idea at the time.'

'A lot of things do,' said Samantha drily. 'It seemed a good idea me getting engaged to Byron. I didn't stop to think it through, to think why he was asking me. I simply grabbed the opportunity.'

'So why don't you stay engaged? Why don't you marry him?' Hell, was she really saying these things? 'Byron won't let you down. And in time, who knows? He'll probably learn to love you just as much as you love him. You needn't be afraid that I'll ever—'

'Danielle!' cried Samantha fiercely. 'I will not change my mind. I shall look on my brief engagement to Byron as a pleasurable interlude in my life. And I expect I shall fall in love with someone else before I know it. Please do not worry about me.'

But Danielle *was* worried, and when she got home she could not get Samantha out of her mind. This beautiful blonde was the most selfless person Danielle had ever met. She could not imagine, if she were in the same position, that she would give up the man she loved so graciously. And she wouldn't mind betting that Samantha was in her hotel room right now, crying her eyes out.

She telephoned Melissa's sister, explaining that she wouldn't be going abroad after all. At least not for a while. 'I am so sorry; I hate doing this to you. I hope I haven't left you in the lurch.'

'Good Lord, Danielle, don't apologise,' Fiona said. 'It can't be helped. I just hope Byron's going to be all right.'

And Melissa said the same when Danielle rang her.

Every day she went to see Byron. Sometimes Samantha was there, sometimes she saw him alone, but nothing was ever said about his engagement being over.

When, a week later, the doctor said that Byron could go home, she and Samantha were delighted. 'So long as there is someone to look after you,' he warned. 'It wouldn't be advisable to return to work or do anything too strenuous. You'll need plenty of rest.'

Samantha's first words when the doctor left the room were, 'I think we have a problem.'

Byron frowned. 'Why?'

'Who's going to look after you? I'm at work all day; I can't do it. I certainly can't take any more time off.'

Byron frowned and began to speak, but Samantha went on heedlessly, 'I think you should spend a few days with Danielle. You'll get good fresh air in your lungs instead of city fumes, you'll be able to go for walks— maybe even a gentle ride on Sandor as you get stronger. In fact you'll be much better off all round.'

'It doesn't sound like a good solution to me,' he said gruffly.

It didn't sound like a good idea to Danielle either. She knew why Samantha had suggested it, and why she had done it like this, while the three of them were together. It was so that she, Danielle, would not be able to say that she did not want this. She was glad that Byron was doing it for her.

'It sounds a perfect solution to me,' said Samantha stubbornly. 'I'm sure you won't mind, Danielle, will you?' Her smile was guileless.

But before Danielle could answer Byron said, 'You're forgetting, Sam, that Danielle has Tony living with her. They won't want me around. As a matter of fact I think that you and I should have a little talk alone. Would you mind, Ellie?'

Danielle did not mind in the least, and as she left the room she mentally crossed her fingers that he would be able to persuade Samantha that it was the worst possible solution. The best thing Byron could do was go home and hire a nurse, or a home help of some sort. It wasn't as if money was a problem.

She caught Sam's eye on the way out and was given an enormous wink, and when Samantha came to find her in the hospital cafeteria she discovered why.

'I've done it,' the blonde girl said.

'Don't you think you should have consulted me first?' asked Danielle. But she wasn't angry with Sam, merely fearful of what lay ahead.

In answer Samantha held out her left hand. Her third finger was bare.

Danielle screamed, and then clapped her hand over her mouth when several pairs of eyes looked in their direction. 'You mean you've done *it?*'

Samantha nodded.

'How did Byron react?' Danielle's tone was hushed now, almost reverent, though she was not aware of it.

'As I expected, he was relieved.'

Danielle's eyes narrowed. 'Are you telling me the truth, Sam?' He would be puzzled, curious, hurt even, but relieved? It would be out of character. He might be relieved privately, if he did not love her, but he would never let Sam see it, he was too much of a gentleman.

'Well, I think he was,' Samantha admitted. 'He wouldn't accept the ring back; he told me to put it in my pocket if I didn't want to wear it. So I took it off straight away. He got the message.'

'What excuse did you give him?'

'That I didn't love him enough, that it was the surprise element that had made me accept, that I thought he didn't really love me either. He didn't deny it.'

'You didn't tell him that—?'

'No, I didn't,' cut in Samantha quickly. 'I kept my word. And I think you'll find that he won't object to your looking after him. It was a pretty good idea of mine, don't you think?' Her grey eyes twinkled mischievously. 'I've promised to get his stuff from the hotel, and you'll have no excuse now for not resolving your problems. He said he'd like to see you. And don't forget to tell him about Tony,'' she added warningly.

It was with some hesitancy that Danielle returned to Byron's room. He was sitting waiting in a chair near the window, watching her as she crossed the room.

'Sam's told you?' were his first words.

Danielle nodded, not really knowing what to say. 'I'm sorry' seemed inadequate. And was she sorry? Or was she relieved? No, not relieved, because it would have solved everything if he had got married. All it had done was complicate matters.

'It came as a shock to me.'

'Yes, it must have done.'

'Did you know she was going to do it?'

'No.' Danielle felt that a little white lie was justified. At least she hadn't known Sam was going to do it this morning.

'It leaves me with one very important question,' he said.

Danielle waited. Her heart began to beat very loudly.

'How is it going to affect you and me?'

CHAPTER TWELVE

'I PROMISED Sam that I'd stay with you for a few days,' Byron told Danielle. 'But that was only to shut her up. It's impossible with my rival on the scene. Tell me, Ellie, did you mean it when you said that you loved me?'

How neatly he had linked the two together. She gave a reluctant, almost indiscernible nod which he would probably have missed had he not been watching her closely. At his invitation she had pulled up a chair next to him, and the light from the window fell full on her face. It wasn't sunny but it was a fairly bright day at the beginning of autumn—the time of year she loved best.

'So what are we going to do about it?'

'About—our love?' she asked huskily.

He nodded, and then screwed up his face in pain. 'Damn, I shouldn't do that.' And a few seconds later, 'Well?'

'There's nothing to be done,' she said.

His lips thinned. 'You mean you refuse to get out of your commitment to Tony?'

Danielle knew that she could not be less than honest. 'There is no commitment. There never was.'

He looked at her in total disbelief. 'I don't understand.'

'He's a friend, that's all,' she said with a guilty grimace. 'He's back in Malaysia now. I think he has a girl over there. I simply gave him a roof over his head for a few nights.'

His frown deepened. 'And you let me think that—?'

165

'It seemed like the best thing to do.'

'Why?' He shot the word at her like a bullet from a gun. 'It makes no sense.'

'It did to me,' she said quietly.

'Was it only when you thought I was going to die that you realised you still loved me?' His eyes locked with hers. 'It's not very flattering, I must admit, but if it is the case—then I'm glad I had the accident.'

Maybe it would be best to let him think that. 'It brought me to my senses,' she agreed with a slow, weak smile.

In contrast Byron's smile was instant and almost split his face in two. 'I can't wait to get out of here. Do you reckon Sam knows how we feel about each other?' He frowned again as another thought struck him. 'Do you think that's why she broke off the engagement? Why she suggested I come to you to convalesce?'

Danielle shrugged. 'Maybe. She's an intuitive girl, and thoughtful. I like her very much. I thought you made a perfect couple.'

'*We* make a better one,' he growled. 'You'd best remember that.' And then, as though the conversation had exhausted him, he slumped back in the chair and closed his eyes.

She stood up. 'I'll go now, Byron.'

He lifted heavy lids. 'You can't leave without kissing me. It's mandatory to kiss the man you love.'

Pulses stampeded. She didn't want to, and yet at the same time she did. She brushed her lips lightly against his cheek, but a surprisingly strong hand clasped the back of her head and guided her mouth over his.

The kiss seemed to last for ever even though Danielle knew it was for no more than a few seconds. It created a whole flood of sensation. How she found the strength to walk out of the room she did not know.

Byron's head felt as though a sledgehammer was being smashed against it; the pain was relentless. But the doctors had said it would go—in time. He must never forget that the falling masonry had cracked his skull. But just how much time did he have to give it?

He had been living with Danielle for almost two weeks. He had said nothing to her of his hopes and aspirations. He had asked nothing of her either. There was time now, all the time in the world. She would never know the enormous relief he had felt when she'd said that Tony meant nothing to her. He had wanted to get up out of his chair and dance—and he would have done, had he been fit enough.

She was looking after him as well as any nurse could. She was attuned to his every mood, seemed to know instinctively when he wasn't feeling well, when he wanted to be alone or when he wanted company.

When she had declared her love that first night she'd come to him in the hospital he'd thought he had died and gone to heaven. And he could see no reason now why they could not get back together permanently.

Gradually he had got stronger, his walks—which had begun with a stroll around the garden—got longer, and his headaches grew less frequent. They still raged sometimes, and his moods then would be filthy, but Danielle ignored them; she was always cheerful and smiling, and if it was possible his love for her grew deeper.

Eventually he decided that the time was right to tell her about John. It had been on his mind for days. He'd had all the facts since before his accident, and he thought she ought to know. He waited until they had finished their evening meal. The curtains were closed and the lights on, and when Danielle began to gather the dishes to take them out to the kitchen he stopped her.

'Leave those for now, Ellie; I'll help you later. There's something I have to tell you. Let's move into the lounge.'

She looked at him warily, and once they were comfortable, he in an armchair, she on the settee opposite, he said, 'You know that the gallery has finally been pulled down?'

Danielle nodded and frowned and looked a bit amazed, as though this was the last thing she had expected him to talk about. 'How did you find out? I tried to keep it from you. I deliberately binned the newspaper it was in. I knew how much it would upset you.'

'It did,' he agreed. 'I made a few phone calls one day when you were out, and I must confess I was gutted. But it was the right thing to do; it was totally unsafe. I'm walking proof of that,' he added wryly.

'You're the luckiest man I know.'

'I'm luckier than John,' he acknowledged. And he was even luckier because Danielle loved him—although they were still carefully steering away from any emotional commitment. He was taking each day as it came, waiting for the right opportunity, as he had been waiting for this one.

'I think you should know,' he said, choosing his words carefully, 'that John was aware that Scotts were taking short-cuts.'

Danielle drew her perfectly arched brows together and tilted her head to one side. 'So if he hadn't died he could have done something about it? Is that what you're saying? I wonder why he never told me. But then he never did discuss work. He didn't bring his work home, nor did he take his private life to work. I suppose in essence he was two different men.'

'The point is he did try to do something,' Byron said quietly. 'He went to Scotts and threatened to take them to court unless they put things right.'

'And?'

Several seconds went by before Byron answered, and when he did there was deep sorrow in his voice. 'He was silenced.'

Her eyes widened and she seemed to stop breathing. 'What are you saying?'

'His death wasn't an accident, Ellie.'

'You mean someone deliberately set out to kill him?'

'Yes, I'm afraid so.'

Danielle clapped her hands to her mouth. 'But the coroner recorded a verdict of accidental death.' Two huge tears spilled out of her eyes and rolled down her cheeks.

He wanted to get up and go to her, he wanted to hold her and console her, but the story wasn't yet told. 'There was a huge cover-up. Rod had his suspicions and went to the police, but they more or less suggested he was being paranoid. And when Scotts found out what he'd done they said that if he made any further allegations *his* life would be in danger too. The poor man's been scared half to death since, afraid to breathe a word. It took me ages to get everything out of him.'

Danielle's eyes reflected her horror, and she shivered. 'You don't think that your accident was—?'

'Heavens, no,' he cut in quickly. 'That was definitely my own fault. I do think, though, that Scotts deliberately disbanded themselves when the first signs of trouble hit the gallery. I think they were running scared.'

'This guy—the one who dropped the bricks on

John—what's happened to him?' Her face was pale, her hands twisting nervously in her lap.

'Nothing's happened yet, but we know where he lives.'

'We?'

'Myself and the private detective I hired,' he told her. 'I intend handing over my evidence. If it hadn't been for this damn accident I would already have done it. I shall not rest until John's murderer is behind bars.' And at last he joined her on the settee, pulling her gently into the crook of his arm. He stroked her hair back from her face. 'I'm sorry I had to tell you about John; I know how much you loved him.'

'I didn't,' she said quietly.

Byron's heart missed a couple of beats before bounding on at an unaccustomed pace. 'But you said…'

'I know what I said,' she returned. 'I liked him, I admired him, I thought a lot of him. We got on well together, and perhaps I did love him after a fashion, but not the way I love you.' This latter was said very quietly, almost as though she did not want him to hear.

'So why did you lie?' he asked quietly.

'Self-protection, I guess.'

'Because you didn't want to admit that you had never stopped loving me?'

'Yes.'

It was the tiniest, quietest yes he had ever heard, but it was enough. He groaned and turned her in his arms so that he could triumphantly claim her mouth.

He could feel his heart pounding in his chest, feel the blood rushing through his veins, and rising above all was an intense physical need. Would Ellie allow it? Was it too soon? Should he curb his desire?

He probed the soft, moist depths of her mouth with

his tongue, he kissed every inch of her face, his hands reacquainted themselves with her softly rounded breasts. Oh, heaven. And when that wasn't enough he undid the buttons on her blouse, unclipped her bra, and then feasted his eyes.

When he stroked his fingers over her sweetly scented skin, when he held the weight of her breasts in his palms, when he brushed his thumbs over her nipples and she drew in her breath in a way he remembered so very, very well, his joy knew no bounds.

He lowered his head and took each nipple in turn into his mouth, sucking, biting, teasing. Lord, she tasted good. He looked up at her face. Her eyes were closed, her head back, her lips parted, her breathing rapid.

And then pain shot through his head and he knew that he had overdone it. Damn! And damn again.

'Byron?'

She knew. As always she was attuned to his every mood, his every thought, almost.

'Your head?'

'I'm sorry.'

'Don't be.' She cradled his head in her lap and laid her hands gently on it, on the soft fuzz of regrowth that was all he had. He could feel the warmth of her touch, the soothing warmth, and as they lay still together the pain gradually went.

And she knew that it had gone. Without him breathing a word, she knew.

Now was the right time to tell him, Danielle thought. While they were close, while he was in a receptive mood—but before they got too close. He wouldn't feel so bad then about walking away from her.

'I have something to tell you too,' she said, stroking

his head, feeling the short hairs beneath her fingers. Actually he looked quite handsome without any hair. Very distinguished. Very sexy in fact.

'If it's not good news I don't want to hear it,' he told her, tilting his head backwards in her lap so that he could look up at her.

He looked funny upside down, but she did not smile. 'It's about why I walked out on you. And I think it's very important that—'

'Ellie!' He stopped her flow of words immediately, then sat up and took her hand into his. 'Ellie, the past is over and done with. I want it put away and not discussed. We have our future before us and I hope—no, indeed, I pray—that it is going to be a happy one. So, please, say no more.'

'But, Byron, you don't understand. I—'

Once again he interjected. 'I do not wish to put myself through any more pain. And nor, I suspect, do you. Do not worry about your conscience; I accept that we both made mistakes. All I'm asking for now is a fresh beginning. Is that too much?'

Danielle sighed. He was blocking her at every turn. It was as though he didn't want to know. And yet it was so important that he did. She would have to wait; perhaps she hadn't chosen her moment well after all.

At the end of the week Danielle made one of her frequent visits to the cemetery. She had told Byron that she was going into Birmingham, and he had wanted to go with her, as he sometimes did. So she had said that she'd a lot of business to discuss with Melissa and he would be in the way and probably totally bored.

As she carefully arranged sprays of delicate pink carnations she told Lucy all about her daddy, and his accident, and the fact that he was living with her for the moment.

When she got home Byron was missing, and she was glad, because her visits always made her sad for a few hours afterwards.

Byron did not believe for one moment that Danielle was going to see Melissa. He did not know why, it was just a gut feeling, and because he was curious he followed her. And when he saw where she went he asked himself why she couldn't have told him that she was going to visit John's grave. He would have understood. It was a perfectly natural thing for her to do.

From a distance he watched as she knelt over the grave and put fresh flowers in the vase. He watched as she bent her head as if in prayer, and he watched as she left. She did not see him; she would not have seen him even if he'd been standing right next to her.

She was in a world of her own and looked unutterably sad. He had never seen her look quite like this before. Had she been lying when she'd said that she had never loved John? Had it been for his benefit? The thought did him no good at all.

Unable to help himself, he took a look at the gravestone, and what he saw shocked him to the core. It wasn't a man's grave, but a child's. A tiny little grave. There was no date. Nothing very much at all. It said simply 'Lucy, treasured baby.'

Danielle and John had had a baby! And like his own it hadn't lived. It had come into the world but...

He went home quickly and Danielle was there; she still looked sad, though she did her best to hide it. He couldn't wait now for a right moment; he had to tell her straight away what he had discovered so that he could comfort her, tell her that she would always have him at her side from now on. No burden had to be borne alone.

'Danielle, I hope you'll forgive me, but I followed you to the cemetery. I had a feeling you weren't going to the shop.'

Every ounce of colour drained from her face and she sat down on one of the kitchen stools as though her legs would no longer hold her.

'I know about the baby. Why didn't you tell me?'

She looked at him long and hard and she tried to hold back her tears, but they escaped and slid down her cheeks. 'I tried, Byron. I wanted to tell you the other day, but you wouldn't listen.'

He frowned then, trying to recall such a conversation. The only time he hadn't listened was when she'd wanted to talk about their break-up.

'I know I should have told you at the time, but I couldn't, I was afraid of—I just couldn't, Byron.'

It suddenly began to dawn on him. 'Are you saying, Ellie…?' he asked slowly. 'Are you saying that Lucy was—*our* child?'

CHAPTER THIRTEEN

DANIELLE nodded. This wasn't the way she had wanted Byron to find out, but she was glad that he had.

'And you were afraid to tell me?'

'I thought you would be angry. I thought you would blame me, the same as you did when I miscarried. You were horrible to me, Byron, and I couldn't go through it again. I...' She didn't even try to stop her tears now. She just looked at him through wet eyes and saw that he was indeed beginning to show signs of anger.

'I'm more angry that you didn't tell me,' he said fiercely. 'I cannot believe that something like this happened and I didn't know about it. Oh, God, this is awful.'

'No more awful than it was for me,' she protested. 'It was the most traumatic experience of my life.' One she had thought she would never get over.

'And I should have been there to share it with you,' he pointed out. 'You should not have had to go through it alone. Dammit, Ellie, I was the father. How do you think that makes me feel now? It was my responsibility as well as yours.'

'Don't shout at me, Byron.' Her face was screwed up in pain. 'I've suffered enough, am still suffering as a matter of fact. Just think about that.'

'You didn't put a date on the grave,' he accused.

'It was in case you ever saw it. I didn't want you to know.'

He winced and looked painfully aggrieved. 'How old was she when...?'

'Just a few hours.'

'Oh, my God.' He paced the kitchen as his mind tried to accept all this disturbing information, and Danielle dropped her head into her hands. She was appalled to think that he had followed her; it just proved that she wasn't a very good liar. But at least he now knew, that was something.

'Danielle.' He suddenly stopped and looked at her. 'Did you actually know you were pregnant when you left me?'

She nodded, feeling guilty now.

'Dammit, why? Shouldn't that have been the time when you needed me?'

'Yes, but I was afraid,' she answered in a choking whisper. 'Afraid that if I lost that baby as well *you* would leave *me*. I knew how much you wanted children. I decided to walk out first, and then when I lost the baby I knew I had done the right thing.'

'That is the most ridiculous thing I have ever heard,' he raged. 'I would not have walked out on you, Ellie. What sort of a monster do you think I am? And when you lost the baby that was exactly the time when you needed me. Why didn't you phone? Why didn't you send for me? At the very least you could have let me know.'

'It seemed the best thing at the time,' she said quietly.

Byron resumed his pacing, and Danielle began to worry that he was upsetting himself too much and that his head would begin to ache. 'I think we should have a cup of tea. Would you mind making it?' Having something to do would help take his mind off the bombshell she had just dropped.

It was over an hour later before the subject was finally exhausted. Byron had wanted to know every single detail, and even Danielle's head had begun to throb by the time he was finished.

'There is one consolation,' he said, and this was long after their conversation—well into the evening in fact. They had been watching a natural history programme on TV about animals born in the wild and their rate of survival, and it must have set him thinking again. 'When we get married we can always try again. And I shall personally make sure that you have the best medical care possible.'

When Danielle broke down in more tears he looked at her in surprise. 'What have I said wrong? Don't you want to marry me, Ellie? Am I taking too much for granted? I know I should have asked, but I thought that since we've both admitted that we love each other it was a foregone conclusion.'

She kept her head turned away from him. 'It's not that I don't want to—but I can't.' And the pain was too much to bear.

'Can't, Ellie?' He touched his fingers to her chin and compelled her to face him. 'Can't?'

She closed her eyes and shook her head.

He tenderly blotted her face with his handkerchief. 'Why?'

'Because—because—' She swallowed with difficulty. Her throat felt knotted, as did her stomach muscles. 'Because, Byron, I could never be a proper wife. I could never a mother. Something happened after I'd had Lucy. I can't—I can't have any more children. Not ever.'

She watched his face carefully, waiting for the dismay, the horror, the rejection. But there was none of those things. Instead there was compassion and warmth, and his only thoughts were for her.

'Oh, my darling, darling Ellie. Did you really think that would matter to me? That it would make any difference to how I feel?' He pulled her gently into his arms. 'I don't care so long as I have you. I love you, Ellie, I love you with all my heart. I always have. My life has been empty all the years we've been apart. And nothing is going to take you away from me again, nothing at all.'

'But you want children. You want a large family.' She looked at him through her tear-misted eyes. 'You've always said that; you told Samantha as well. She's quite prepared to give you as many babies as you like. You'd do better marrying her.'

He settled her comfortably against him. 'The only reason I asked Sam to marry me was because I thought you were lost to me for ever,' he told her quietly. 'I won't deny that I'm fond of her, and she's wonderful company, but I didn't ask her simply so that I could have children. I guess it was a rebound thing, really. The marriage would have worked, the same as yours and John's did, but it wouldn't have had the spark that lights *our* lives.'

Danielle wasn't so sure. 'The blouse—you bought that for her, and it was going to be underwear,' she accused.

His mouth twisted. 'The lingerie was going to be for you, if the time was ever right. In point of fact it was an excuse to come and see you for one last time, except that I didn't feel I could walk out without buying something. The reason I gave Samantha the blouse was because she had nothing to wear—or so she said. You know what you women are like. It didn't mean a thing.

'I used her, and I hate myself for it. When she brought my suitcase to the hospital I told her that I felt guilty, but she said I had nothing to chastise myself for. She seemed to understand.'

'That's because,' said Danielle, 'she knew the way things were between you and me.'

His brows rose in surprise. 'She did?'

'Yes.'

'And so she left the scene. What a remarkable girl.'

'Indeed she is,' agreed Danielle.

'I shall have to find a way to make it up to her. But we're getting off the subject of you and me. If you thought the fact that you can't have children would turn me against you, then you don't know me very well at all.'

'You wouldn't mind?' Faint hope began to rise.

'Of course I damn well wouldn't mind. It's you I love, you funny little idiot. You. I want you with me for the rest of my life.'

'I suppose we could adopt.'

'Maybe we'll talk about it,' he said. 'But do you know what I think we should do now? I think we should go to bed. Together. I think the time has come, don't you?'

Danielle smiled and nodded. Every last doubt had been lifted. She felt wonderfully, magnificently free. No weight on her shoulders, no worries, no fears. Byron loved her for what she was.

She ought to have known. She ought to have known he wouldn't be narrow-minded enough to let her infertility affect him. And she had meant what she'd said about adoption, because no matter how much he declared that he didn't mind about children she knew that deep down inside it was what he wanted.

The following morning, after a night of the best love-making Danielle could ever remember, a night that would live in her mind for ever, a night when Byron had taken her to heights undreamt of, she had a phone call from her mother.

'Where are you?' she asked, imagining Evelyn phoning from some exotic port.

'We're home. I've suffered the most dreadful seasickness, and I couldn't take any more. I've just discovered that you didn't go to America after all.'

'No, I didn't, because Byron—'

'Yes, I know,' her mother cut in. 'Rod rang the office and they told him about the accident. Is he all right?'

'He's getting better,' Danielle said. 'I'll come and see you after breakfast. As a matter of fact I have some good news. No, you'll have to wait.'

She turned to Byron. 'The newlyweds are home. Mother's been terribly seasick.'

'Poor Evelyn,' he said, looking suitably sympathetic. 'And what was it you didn't do because of me?'

Trust him to pick up on that, she thought. 'Go to America.'

'*What?*'

She laughed at his startled expression. 'I couldn't face the thought of being invited to your wedding, so I decided to take myself off for a year. I was all packed when I read about your accident. Another few hours and I'd have been out of the country.'

He shuddered, and gathered her to him. 'Thank God for small mercies.'

She nodded. 'I've thanked Him a lot of times myself.'

He kissed her fiercely, and it was ages before he let her go. Then he said, 'Are we supposed to be visiting your mother?'

'As soon as we've eaten.'

'And what sort of food would you like, my adorable Ellie?'

She could not answer because his lips were on hers again, and it was almost lunchtime before they finally left the house.

Evelyn was surprised to see Byron with Danielle, but she made none of her usual caustic comments, asking instead how he was. And Rod looked deeply concerned as well.

'What a shame you had to cut your honeymoon short,' Danielle said sympathetically. 'You poor thing, Mother. It must have been dreadful.'

'Don't get her started.' Rod had a twinkle in his eyes. 'I've had it all the way home. What would you like to drink, Danielle? Wine? A Scotch for you, Byron?'

Byron looked at Danielle, and she looked at him. 'I think,' he said, 'that champagne might be more in order. And as a matter of fact I have a bottle right here.' He produced it with a flourish from behind his back.

'We're getting married,' Danielle announced, her wide smile and her shining eyes giving away her inner happiness.

Evelyn shrieked, and then, to Danielle's total amazement, said, 'I'm pleased for you, Danielle.' And to Byron, 'I was wrong about you. I'll be proud to have you as my son-in-law—again.'

And Rod, after asking what had happened to Samantha, added his congratulations. The champagne was opened and toasts drunk, and afterwards, while Danielle was helping her mother with lunch, Evelyn said, 'I want to apologise, Danielle, for all the times I refused to let Byron speak to you. He phoned more often than I ever told you, and he called round in person so many times. I am truly sorry. I thought I was doing the right thing.'

In her present frame of mind Danielle was prepared

to forgive her mother anything. She should have known that Byron would not let her walk away that easily.

The afternoon passed quickly, each person with stories to tell, and it was not until they were on their way home that Danielle told Byron what her mother had said. 'I had no idea you'd tried so many times to speak to me.'

His smile was wry. 'I'm glad it was Evelyn stopping me, and not you. I really did think that you'd grown to hate me.'

'I could never hate you,' she declared firmly.

'That's a relief.' He reached out and touched her hand. 'It's been on my mind for so long.'

'Don't even think about it again,' she said. 'I've always loved you, Byron. It's something that will never go away.'

'You may kiss the bride.'

It was the happiest day in Danielle's life. Marrying Byron the first time had been good, but this surpassed it. They were each sure now of their feelings. They had gone through so much that they knew nothing could ever part them again.

The kiss lasted so long that the vicar cleared his throat to remind them that everyone was waiting. Samantha's eyes were moist as she watched them, but Tony had been unable to come. He'd sent his best wishes, and said that he was glad she was doing the right thing at last. And, of course, Evelyn cried in the customary fashion of all brides' mothers.

After the wedding reception they flew away on their honeymoon to St Lucia.

'Happy?' Byron asked as they lay together in a swinging hammock in front of his beach house.

'How could I not be?' she wanted to know. 'This has

to be the most perfect place in the world.' White sand, blue skies, swaying palm trees. She could ask for nothing more.

'I think I agree,' he said. 'It more than makes up for not having had a honeymoon first time around, don't you think?'

'Absolutely.' She twisted the slim gold band on her finger—her old wedding ring, which she had insisted on wearing. Byron had been amazed that she'd kept it and had wanted to buy her a new one, something far better, but she had remained adamant. This, to her, was a symbol of their love.

'I love you so much, Mrs Meredith.'

'And I love you, Mr Meredith. I've been lying here thinking how lucky I am. I was also wondering where we are going to live when we go home.'

Everything had happened with such lightning speed that they hadn't even discussed it. She did not in all honesty want to sell up, though if Byron insisted they live in London then that was what she would do. Wherever he was happy, she would be happy too.

'I think we should keep both homes going.'

She smiled widely. 'What an excellent idea, Mr Meredith. I'm so glad I've married a wealthy man.'

He gave her a playful dig in the ribs. 'Maybe we should go back to our little terraced house?'

Danielle shook her head at once, shuddering at the thought. 'There are too many bad memories.'

'Oh, I don't know, there are some good ones as well. I promise you now, though, Mrs Meredith, that nothing will spoil our happiness in future.'

It was sealed with a kiss, and Danielle knew that he would never break it. That she would be happy with Byron for as long as she lived.

EPILOGUE

'MUMMY, Daddy, watch me.'

Danielle and Byron were filled with pride as three-year-old Grace took her little pony over a low jump. It was only a few inches high—the pony could stride over it, really—but Grace thought it was wonderful, and Danielle clapped with delight. 'Clever girl, Grace.'

'Me ride, me ride.' Two-year-old Luke, sitting on his father's shoulders, jigged up and down with excitement. Even Champ, their golden retriever, looked excited.

'In a moment, darling,' said Danielle. 'Let Grace finish first.'

At the moment the children were sharing a pony, but Byron had said only the other day that he thought they should buy another one. Both children were showing a remarkable aptitude for riding, and Byron himself was also now something of an expert. Or so he kept telling Danielle.

Although Byron had said that he didn't mind about not having children, Danielle had seen the change in him when they'd adopted Grace two years into their marriage, and, a year later, Luke. He was a contented man now. He had been happy before, not once had he said anything to her, but she had always sensed that there was something missing in his life.

And today she had some astonishing news for him. She waited until they were alone, until the children were taking their afternoon sleep.

'Do you believe in miracles, Byron?'

'Indisputably. It was a miracle I married you again, Ellie. All my hopes and prayers answered.'

'I think I might be able to answer another prayer,' she said quietly.

He frowned and he pushed his hair back from his forehead, his thick, wiry hair, which was laced with a lot of grey. Danielle recalled his well-shaped bald head after the accident, and how sexy she had thought it. Now she thought his grey hair was sexy. In fact he was still one very sexy man.

'So go on, Ellie, tell me what amazing thing has happened.'

'Do you remember we once said we'd like four children?'

He nodded and then groaned. 'You're not planning on adopting another couple? I couldn't face the sleepless nights. I'm getting too old for that game.'

'So—if I told you that I was pregnant—that as a matter of fact I'm having twins—then you wouldn't be delighted?'

He stared at her long and hard. Then he shouted out with sheer joy and swung her round in his arms. 'You're not kidding me, Ellie?'

She shook her head. 'I'm perfectly serious. The doctor phoned me this morning to confirm the results. He's baffled as to how I got pregnant, but there it is. It's happened.' And was it any wonder given the number of times they made love? In all the five years they had been married Byron had never tired of her. Nor she of him.

'Oh, my God. You'll have to be careful, Ellie. You'll have to rest a lot. I'll do everything; I'll look after you, my darling. This is wonderful.' Tears came to his eyes. 'This is all I've ever hoped for—more, in fact. Oh, my sweet, I do love you.'

Seeing her man cry made Danielle cry too, and it was a long time before there was a dry eye in the house.

'It's a boy!' said the midwife. And, minutes later, 'It's a girl!' Two tiny babies who both looked incredibly like their father, except that the girl had red hair.

And when Danielle took them home a few days later Byron was the proudest father alive. He'd already made plans for the future. They'd already bought a bigger house, and they would need more horses—more of everything in fact.

The only thing they didn't need any more of, could not have found room for, was love. Their cup had finally run over.

Three brothers, one
tuxedo…and one destiny!

Date With Destiny

A brand-new anthology from
USA TODAY bestselling author

KRISTINE ROLOFSON
MURIEL JENSEN
KRISTIN GABRIEL

The package said "R. Perez" and
inside was a tuxedo. But which
Perez brother—Rick, Rafe or
Rob—was it addressed to? This
tuxedo is on a mission…to lead
each of these men to the altar!

DATE WITH DESTINY
will introduce you to
the characters of
Forrester Square…
an exciting new continuity
starting in August 2003.

LEGACIES. LIES. LOVE.

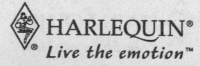
HARLEQUIN®
Live the emotion™

Visit us at www.eHarlequin.com

PHDWD

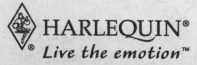

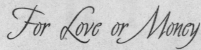

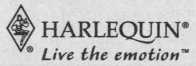

BETTY NEELS

Harlequin Romance® is proud to present this delightful story by Betty Neels. This wonderful novel is the climax of a unique career that saw Betty Neels become an international bestselling author, loved by millions of readers around the world.

A GOOD WIFE
(#3758)

Ivo van Doelen knew what he wanted—he simply needed to allow Serena Lightfoot time to come to the same conclusion. Now all he had to do was persuade Serena to accept his convenient proposal of marriage without her realizing he was already in love with her!

Don't miss this wonderful novel— brought to you by Harlequin Romance®!

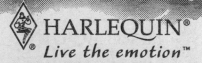

HARLEQUIN®
Live the emotion™

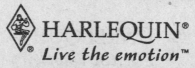

The world's bestselling romance series.

HARLEQUIN®
Presents

Seduction and Passion Guaranteed!

Coming soon...
To the rescue...armed with a ring!

Modern-Day Knights

Marriage is their mission!

Look out for more stories of
Modern-Day Knights...

Coming next month:
NATHAN'S CHILD
by Anne McAllister
#2333

Coming in August
AT THE SPANIARD'S PLEASURE
by Jacqueline Baird
#2337

Pick up a Harlequin Presents® novel and you will enter a world of spine-tingling passion and provocative, tantalizing romance!

Available wherever Harlequin books are sold.

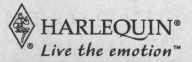

HARLEQUIN®
Live the emotion™